bar down

Cover Design by Emily Silver

Editing by Happily Editing Anns

Formatting by 3Beansbooks

www.authoremilysilver.com

BAR DOWN

A Nashville Knights Novel

EMILY SILVER

To the Emily of five years ago who was nervous as hell to publish her first book.

Here we are, 30 books later.

Here's to the next 30 and next five years…

Prologue

MUSIC CITY MATCHES

New message from Music City Matches user TheFriendlyGhost at 9:17pm

THEFRIENDLYGHOST

Are you a cat? Because I'm feline a connection between us

CATSRCOOL

Does that actually work?

No. But it broke the ice 😉

Oh my God. I should end this right now

You won't

You sound pretty confident there

Because you're going to tell me why cats are cool instead

If I have to tell you, you're clearly a dog person

I love dogs. Don't have one, but I grew up with them. Never had a cat though

Cats are better. They have an air of mystery about them

Are you saying dogs don't?

You know exactly what dogs are thinking all the time

But not cats

Nope. Hence the mystery

And you like a little mystery?

Coming from the ghost

Are you going to ghost me?

Why would you think that?

Your username??

If you knew my name, you'd get it

What's your name?

Are you going to tell me yours?

I don't think you've earned it yet

Ouch. How do I earn it?

Tell me something no one knows about you

I hate hockey

Hockey? Really? That's not that exciting

If you knew what I did, it would be

What do you do?

I play hockey

Aren't you funny

I know

I have to run

Don't ghost me

Same can be said for you

New message from Music City Matches user CatsRCool at 11:11am

CATSRCOOL

What's the worst pick-up line you've ever used on someone?

THEFRIENDLYGHOST

Are you a cat? Because I'm feline a connection between us

Not the one you used on me

But it was!

Have you never used a pickup line before?

Never

And you started with me? Ballsy

Something about you made me want to try it out

And? Would you try it again?

Never again

I mean, not one that bad

Okay, if you had to use a pickup line to try and woo me, what would you use?

Woo you?

Why am I trying to woo you?

You know what I mean

Might need a dictionary

Didn't realize we were time traveling tonight

Let's flip a coin. Heads, I'm yours. Tails, you're mine.

Damn. I like it!

<<taking a bow gif>> Thank you, thank you

You would've won me over if I needed it

If?

I already won you over instead with my feline connection

Did you though?

You're still talking to me, aren't you?

New message from Music City Matches user TheFriendlyGhost at 8:31am

THEFRIENDLYGHOST

Tell me something no one else knows about you

CATSRCOOL

I hate music

You hate...music?

What do you listen to in the car?

Podcasts

On why cats are cool

Maybe I should find you one on ghosts then

Wouldn't that just be a crime podcast?

Nah

They're already unalived

Well I don't do crime

Really?

Nope. I need happy things

Like cats

Like cats

New message from Music City Matches user CatsRCool at 3:42pm

CATSRCOOL

If you could have dinner with any person, living or dead, who would it be?

THEFRIENDLYGHOST

Wayne Gretzky

I should have known that would be your answer

Then why'd you ask?

What if it was someone interesting, like Freddie Mercury?

Hey! He's interesting

I take it Queen is your answer?

Not Queen, Freddie

Freddie Mercury is the greatest musician of all time

I will take no criticism on this

Ever.

Point made

I guess I shouldn't make fun of you then for picking the obvious answer

I guess you shouldn't

I'd love to learn more about hockey from him

Other than passing the ball?

You did NOT just say that!

Just wanted to see your reaction

You made it too easy

New message from Music City Matches user TheFriendlyGhost at

8:18pm

THEFRIENDLYGHOST

If you could watch any movie again for the first time, what would it be and why?

CATSRCOOL

Movies? Damn

I don't know if I can choose…

You have to

Five…

Four…

Three…

Fine! Ten Things I Hate About You

You're mean

No way

I love that movie!

Seriously?

What, I can't like a rom-com?

You don't seem like the rom-com kinda guy

And what kind of guy do I seem like then?

Documentaries about books

Documentaries

About books

Is that really what you think of me?

Well, maybe about hockey

So you can learn how to pass the puck

At least you're improving and know it's a puck

And it's played on a field with quarters

You wound me

Maybe you need to watch a hockey documentary

With you? Sure

Consider it a date then

New message from Music City Matches user CatsRCool at 12:02pm

CATSRCOOL

If you could be a dinosaur, what kind of dinosaur would you be?

THEFRIENDLYGHOST

Umm, what?

Dinosaur. What kind?

I've never thought about it

Think about it. I want to know

Will this earn me your name?

Grizabella

It's fine if you don't want to tell me your name

It's from the musical Cats

Cats are so cool they have their own musical?

Yes! It's why cats are superior beings

I'll take your word for it, Bella

Grizabella

Grizabella sounds too mean for you. Bella it is

Okay, Casper

Damn. You guessed my name

<<takes bow>> thank you

Back to the dinosaur question...

What kind of dinosaur would you be?

Triceratops

Really?

Yup. I like their horns

Let me guess. You'll be a T-rex?

Nope.

Seriously? I thought all guys wanted to be a T-rex. Top of the food chain and all that

Not this guy

So you've obviously thought about this then

Only in the last 5 minutes

Pterodactyl

You want to fly then?

Who wouldn't? That'd be badass

Are you a badass in real life, Casper?

Eh, maybe

That's a no 😏

Hey 👻

You only wish you were as cool as this badass

I'll let you know if we ever meet

You want to meet?

Maybe?

Maybe? Wow, I must be wooing you with my dinosaur talk

As scintillating as it is, I have to go

See ya, Casper

Bye, Bella

New message from Music City Matches user TheFriendlyGhost at 11:05pm

THEFRIENDLYGHOST

How do you feel about Julie Andrews?

CATSRCOOL

How do I feel about Julie Andrews?

What kind of question is that?

She's a national treasure

Even though she's from the UK?

Blasphemy!

I'm not lying

It doesn't mean she can't also be our
national treasure

Why are you bringing up Julie Andrews?

The Princess Diaries is on TV

I didn't imagine you watching that

What, I can't watch it?

Just didn't figure you'd like it

My grandma was a big fan of The Sound of
Music

Loved Dame Julie, as she liked to call her

She called her Dame Julie?

Technically she is a Dame

Said it's the least she's owed by all of us

I want to meet your grandma

Before me?

I mean, your grandma sounds like a badass

I want to discuss Dame Julie's best movies
with her

She was

She would have liked you

I mean, not as much as Dame Julie

She didn't even like me that much

And I was her favorite grandkid

Do you sing about your favorite things with her?

No

But I never claimed to be as cool as Dame Julie

Is anyone??

I mean, you're pretty cool

Not Dame Julie cool

You're pretty high up there

Suck up

What can I say?

I was always the teacher's pet

And I was the one that acted out in class

Maybe this is why we matched

They do say opposites attract

Even if we do have pretty good taste in movies

Agreed. #DameJulie4Life

New message from Music City Matches user TheFriendlyGhost at 2:47am

THEFRIENDLYGHOST

Coffee or tea?

CATSRCOOL

Why are you messaging me so early?

Why are you awake?

You're the one messaging me

Too amped up to sleep

And coffee or tea would help with that?

It got me thinking. Everyone has a
preference. What's yours?

Neither

Kombucha

Cats and kombucha. I think I just learned
everything I need to know about you

And?

And what?

Do you like me?

It all hinges on one question

Hit me

Do you like ice cream?

What kind of question is that? Of course I
like ice cream

Well you don't drink coffee, so I was
worried there for a minute

Favorite flavor?

Strawberry

Mine too. With chocolate jimmies

I'm learning so much about you right now

Like what?

Like where you're from

How do you guess that?

You called sprinkles jimmies

You have to be from Mass

Wrong

New Hampshire?

Why do you want to know where I'm from?
It's not like I live there

I like talking to you

I do too. But I'm not asking where
you're from

Detroit

Except Nashville has been home for the last
twenty years

From Motown to Music City

Nashville has only been home for me for
like half that

Which makes me wonder how old
you are…

It's a shame I didn't go into music 💀

Artfully dodging the question

Alright, I'll play your game. What kind of
music would you have gone into?

Jazz

Like saxophones and trumpets jazz?

Yup. My grandpa always played old records
for me growing up and I loved it

Can't carry a tune to save my life

Did you try playing in school?

I did. Lasted one year

Aww. I'm sorry

For the record, I think Casper would make a
wicked cool jazz musician

How are you not from Mass?!

New message from Music City Matches user CatsRCool at 7:59pm

CATSRCOOL

What would our first date be?

THEFRIENDLYGHOST

The first date that never seems to want to
happen?

That one

I don't think you're a dinner and movie kind
of girl

Picked up on that, have you?

Easy thing to pick up on

Have you planned something?

Maybe...

Tell me!

I want to know!

And ruin the surprise?

Nah, I just need to keep you on your toes

Not cool

If you were going to take me on a first date, where would you take me?

Hockey game

Funny

I think I am 😏

I'd take you bowling

Bowling?

What do you have against bowling?

Beer? Bar snacks? Sending a ball flying down the lane to crash into things? Peeping how cute your butt is...I love it!

Checking out my ass already?

Maybe...

Well, there goes our first date

Don't be a stick-in-the-mud!

Not a stick-in-the-mud

I was going to take you bowling

<<hysterical laughter gif>>

Stop it! You were not

I was

For all of the above named reasons

Checking out my ass already? 😏

Turnabout is fair play

Guess we need to go bowling then

New message from Music City Matches user TheFriendlyGhost at 7:27pm

THEFRIENDLYGHOST

Favorite board game?

CATSRCOOL

Board game? Really?

Why do you keep making fun of me?

You make it easy, Casper

You're lucky I like you

I'm honored

Monopoly

Monopoly? Really?

What's wrong with Monopoly?

It's only the longest game ever

I have an older brother and I always
beat him

Made it more fun

Maybe I can convince you it's worth playing

Does this mean you finally want to meet?

Jury's still out

Fun fact about me. I want to do jury duty so
badly

Me too!

Really? I haven't met anyone else that does

It's fascinating. I never get picked and
would love to be on one

I never get picked either. Something about
people recognizing me

What do you do?

I told you. I play hockey. Not my fault if you
don't believe me

It's not my fault I can't see a ghost on
the ice

I'm too fast

Lightning fast

Speaking of. Gotta go

Bye, Casper

Bye, Bella

*New message from Music City Matches user TheFriendlyGhost at
9:17am*

THEFRIENDLYGHOST

One place in the world you want to visit

CATSRCOOL

Switzerland

Huh

Huh, what?

I figured it'd be somewhere tropical

Stick me in a cabin in the Alps in the middle
of winter and I'm a happy gal

Duly noted

Would you sing some songs while you're
there?

Why would you ask me that?

Odd question

Didn't you say you love Julie Andrews?

I'm not making that up

Oh yeah

Sorry, tired from yesterday

Then yes, I would be belting out some "The
Hills are Alive"

Maybe even some "Edelweiss"

Just don't fall down the mountainside

I think you'll need to come with me to make
sure that doesn't happen

I've never been to Switzerland

We'll make a trip out of it

Go over Christmas

See the lights

Is this before or after our bowling date?

Would be a pretty epic first date if we went
to Switzerland

One for the books

Lots of cheese to eat

I bet that fondue goes down pretty smooth
with some Swiss beer

Do you ski?

I wish I could, but I've never tried

I would rock the hell out of hanging in the
lodge by the fire drinking spiked hot
chocolate

You don't actually need to ski for that

You can stay at your little cabin in the Alps
and cozy up by the fire

Now this sounds like a great plan

I wish I could leave right now

If only...

One place in the world you want to
visit now

I'm changing mine to Switzerland

You would say that

What was it before?

Hawaii

Need to tan all that's invisible

Funny

I think I am

Why Hawaii?

I want to lie by the pool with a drink in my hand and not have to worry about a thing

Why not the beach?

I don't like sand

Of course you don't

Why not go to Florida then?

You can find a pool here in Nashville

But I want to go to Hawaii

I want those little pineapple cookies

What pineapple cookies?

They're shortbread cookies in the shape of pineapples

I want to sit by the pool with a pina colada and eat them and not have a care in the world

Can I come with you?

I want that too

Before or after Switzerland?

After

We'll throw in a first date of bowling while we're there

Perfect

New message from Music City Matches user TheFriendlyGhost at 7:10am

THEFRIENDLYGHOST

I'm assuming you like winter since you want to stay in a cabin in the Alps in the middle of winter?

CATSRCOOL

Definitely not a summer girl

I mean, who likes Nashville summers?

It can get pretty miserable

Then why don't you move?

Can't

My job requires me to be here

Until I retire, I'm stuck here

New message from Music City Matches user TheFriendlyGhost at 4:03pm

THEFRIENDLYGHOST

<<photo of a dinosaur>> Thought of you today

Went with my friends' kids to the museum

They told me I'd be a T-rex because I'm so tall

When I told them I want to fly, they said I couldn't

Reminded me of something you would tell me

You there, Bella?

...

New message from Music City Matches user TheFriendlyGhost at 3:57pm

THEFRIENDLYGHOST

Saw a board game cafe in Vancouver

No Monopoly though. We can't go there

Well, maybe we could if you'd answer me

New message from Music City Matches user TheFriendlyGhost at 8:42am

THEFRIENDLYGHOST

Do I need to send out a search party for you?

Although, how would I send out a search party for someone I've never met?

We really need to rectify this soon, Bella

New message from Music City Matches user TheFriendlyGhost at 1:17am

THEFRIENDLYGHOST

You okay, Bella?

New message from Music City Matches user CatsRCool at 5:37am

CATSRCOOL

Didn't mean to ghost you, Casper

You're back

You okay?

I've been busy

Talk to me

Why is it easier to want to tell everything to a stranger on the internet?

Not a stranger

You know what I mean

I'm onto you. Talk to me

I'm exhausted

I was hoping this problem would be solved, but it doesn't look like it's going to be anytime soon

Need me to ruffle some feathers on your behalf?

"Dear Sir, You don't know me, but I know Bella and you need to give her a break. Signed, a fictional ghost"

I'm a real ghost

<<spit laughing gif>>

Thanks for putting a smile on my face

It's what I'm here for

Sorry I haven't been around

It's okay

I wish my life wasn't so hectic

You really can't tell people you need a break?

Can you?

Come play hockey

I wouldn't last one second on the ice

I'll teach you in the offseason

It's great not having to worry about anything

Don't rub it in

Maybe I should take up hockey

I bet you'd look real cute in a helmet, Bella
<<sticker of a cat playing hockey>>

OMG! Where did you find that?

I can't reveal all my secrets

Guess I found you too <<sticker of hockey playing ghost>>

Damn. I guess my real identity has been discovered

The mystery has died. Guess this is the end of our relationship

It was good while it lasted. G2G Bye

Oh. My. God. How old are you?!

Who says G2G?!

You should respect your elders 😜

Not when they say G2G 😅

It really is the end of our relationship

How do the cool kids sign off these days?

Peace out? Goodbye? Actually ghost you?

Hey, Casper?

Yeah?

Thank you

I'm always here for you, Bella

Quinn. My name is Quinn.

Nice to meet you, Quinn. Jasper

Jasper, the friendly ghost

The friendliest

Thank you

anything for you

New message from Music City Matches user CatsRCool at 2:32pm

CATSRCOOL

Have you ever been in love?

THEFRIENDLYGHOST

Coming back swinging, aren't ya?

Gotta make up for ghosting you

So you ask if I've ever been in love?

Would you rather I ask about the weather?

Weather's been shit lately

I can't with you, Jasper

I like you using my actual name, Quinn

Me too

Stop dodging the question

Picked up on that?

You're very easy to read

Sigh…I think I have?

You think?

How can you not know if you've been in love?

Well, when we broke up, I wasn't all that sad about it, even though we'd been dating for three years

I figure if I really loved her, I would have been more upset

I guess that's fair

That was the longest relationship I've had

What about you?

Yes

I've had my heart broken in many ways

Haven't we all?

I wouldn't wish it on anyone

Want to talk about it?

Not really

Want me to change the subject? (Even though you're the one that brought this subject up...)

Way to call a girl out!

Favorite color

Yellow

You?

And you can't say black!

Uhh...

I knew it!

Fine

Green

Don't sound so pained to say that

Are you my neighbor hearing my groans
through the walls?

Okay, this took a turn now…

Head out of the gutter, Bella!

You started it!

Maybe I need to cut this off

And on that note, I have to go

I think you took the longest to scare off 😕

I don't scare that easy, Quinn

New message from Music City Matches user CatsRCool at 4:14am

CATSRCOOL

If you could have any superpower, what
would it be?

THEFRIENDLYGHOST

Is this what your brain thinks about this
early in the morning?

Answer the question

Flying

I should have known, Jasper

Because I'm a ghost?

And because you'd be a pterodactyl

Fair

What about you, Quinn?

Too much to say invisible?

You want to sneak in and out of places without anyone knowing who you are?

You're right. Too much

Super strength then

You can't change it now

I make the rules to this game, so I can do whatever I want

I feel like there is a lot to unpack

No unpacking of anything

Super strength is my superpower

Whatever you say, Quinn

G2G, bye!

Peace out

New message from Music City Matches user CatsRCool at 3:00pm

CatsRCool: Do you ever wish you could be something else?

Something else? Or someone else?

Something. Like a tree

Why would you want to be a tree?

They just sway in the wind

Like nothing ever bothers them

You don't have to be a tree to not let
anything bother you

But they have it so easy

Until a storm comes in and blows
them over

This took a dire turn

It's true! Look at that storm we had here
last week

I wasn't here

Where were you?

Plotting your downfall

Then who would you talk about being a
tree with

Sigh...I guess

What's a tree's favorite dating app?

Omg, stop it!

Timber

Why do trees hate riddles?

Why?

Because they get stumped

Do you have kids? Because you've got the
dad jokes

No kids. My friends' kids though love
telling me bad jokes

Is there where you learned tree jokes?

I just looked them up to impress you

Are you impressed?

Unbe-leaf-ably

QUINN WITH THE JOKES!

Only for you

New message from Music City Matches user TheFriendlyGhost at 1:17am

THEFRIENDLYGHOST

Tell me something you hate

CATSRCOOL

Why?

No one ever talks about what they hate

Because it's bad vibes?

I hate cereal

Cereal? Really?

Frosted Flakes is my guilty pleasure

At least it's not something like Raisin Bran

Gross. Who likes raisins?

I assume old people. Like you

Now, now, Casper. That is not very friendly

Neither is calling me old

I never claimed to be friendly

I thought you said cats were friendly

I said dogs were

Although, I'm pretty sure I said you always
knew what they were thinking

Clearly you're a cat because I never know
what you're thinking

<<cat licking paw gif>>

Tell me something you hate

You

You wound me, old man 😿

Brussels sprouts

😿 😿

I stand by my earlier statement

Brussels sprouts? Really?

What? They're actually gross. Unlike cereal

Have you actually tried them? Like really
tried them?

They're soggy and uninspired

Soggy and uninspired

Are you a judge on a cooking show?

They have no taste

Not mine. Mine are amazing

So whenever we get to meet, you're going to make them for me?

Yes

If we're trying things, I'm bringing you cereal

I walked into that 🙃

New message from Music City Matches user CatsRCool at 11:41pm

CATSRCOOL

Tell me something you love

THEFRIENDLYGHOST

These conversations with you

Tell me something you love

These conversations with you

New message from Music City Matches user TheFriendlyGhost at 9:42am

THEFRIENDLYGHOST

I want to meet you.

Please.

Quinn?

Bella?

{Draft} CatsRCool: I don't know. I don't want you to meet me and hate me because I never told you who I was. I want to meet you more than anything because messaging with you these last few months has kept me from completely losing it. Music used to be my escape, and now it's you. You've kept me together and all I want to do is meet you. Even though I know who you are, Casper.

{Draft} CatsRCool: Jasper Hayes. Starting forward for the Nashville Knights. I used to watch you play hockey with my brother before everything in my life went up in flames.

{Draft} CatsRCool: I hate that I know you hate hockey. I've watched you play now. Since knowing who you are. I can see it in your eyes. The way you're tired. The way you've lost your love of the game.

{Draft} CatsRCool: Because it wasn't always like this. You used to have the same passion for your sport like I did for music.

{Draft} CatsRCool: Before everything good was sucked away.

{Draft} CatsRCool: And what we have now, Jasper, is good.

{Draft} CatsRCool: And I don't want to lose it. I'm scared. Too scared because it seems nothing good in my life lasts anymore. And you're too good to lose, Jasper Hayes.

New message from Music City Matches user CatsRCool at 11:59am

CATSRCOOL

Sorry, Casper. My schedule is too hectic these next few weeks

Maybe when life calms down

THEFRIENDLYGHOST

When will that be?

Soon?

{Draft} TheFriendlyGhost: Soon? Really? I doubt it'll
be soon
{Draft} TheFriendlyGhost: More like never
{Draft} TheFriendlyGhost: Because you're scared, Quinn.
I know you are.
{Draft} TheFriendlyGhost: Whether you like it or not, I
know you.
{Draft} TheFriendlyGhost: Why don't you want to meet?
{Draft} TheFriendlyGhost: Are you worried you won't like
the real me?
{Draft} TheFriendlyGhost: Are you worried I won't like
the real you?
{Draft} TheFriendlyGhost: How could I not like the real
you when I'm pretty sure I'm in love with this version
of you?
{Draft} TheFriendlyGhost: How could I not be after
talking with you for months?
{Draft} TheFriendlyGhost: I've never spent this much time
getting to know someone
{Draft} TheFriendlyGhost: All I want is to see you
{Draft} TheFriendlyGhost: To look into your eyes and
know it's you
{Draft} TheFriendlyGhost: The one who tells me
I'm old
{Draft} TheFriendlyGhost: And weird because I don't like
Brussels sprouts
{Draft} TheFriendlyGhost: And is the only person who
knows how much I hate hockey

{Draft} TheFriendlyGhost: Maybe our paths have already crossed and you thought I didn't notice you?
{Draft} TheFriendlyGhost: I would notice you in any room, Bella
{Draft} TheFriendlyGhost: When someone knows someone the way we know each other, how would we not know each other if we were in the same room?
{Draft} TheFriendlyGhost: Please don't shut me out, Quinn
{Draft} TheFriendlyGhost: Let me in

New message from Music City Matches user TheFriendlyGhost at 12:12pm

THEFRIENDLYGHOST

Soon, then.

{Draft} CatsRCool: Please don't hate me, Jasper
{Draft} CatsRCool: I don't know if I could handle you hating me
{Draft} CatsRCool: I want to meet you more than anything, but how?
{Draft} CatsRCool: How?
{Draft} CatsRCool: I keep coming back to that question above all else
{Draft} CatsRCool: How?
{Draft} CatsRCool: I want you to spot me from across a crowded room and know immediately it's me
{Draft} CatsRCool: Because you'll look at me and know I hate cereal

{Draft} CatsRCool: And love cats more than dogs
{Draft} CatsRCool: And used to play Monopoly with my brother
{Draft} CatsRCool: I want you to bring me kombucha
{Draft} CatsRCool: Tell me I don't have to keep going down this path
{Draft} CatsRCool: I want you to take me into your arms and run
{Draft} CatsRCool: Run as far as we can from this life
{Draft} CatsRCool: I only want you, Jasper
{Draft} CatsRCool: But how?

New message from Music City Matches user CatsRCool at 1:21pm

CATSRCOOL

Why did the cat go to the ghost's house?

THEFRIENDLYGHOST

Why?

Because it heard about the purr-anormal activity

Chapter One

"Hey old man. You think you're gonna get any more ice time tonight?"

"Or are you benched because of that pass?"

"I'd bench him."

I grind my teeth as the game carries on around me, doing my best to ignore the fans heckling me from behind the glass.

One bad pass and they won't shut up.

Fans. They all have opinions about everything. One good game and you're their favorite player. One bad game and you'll never hear the end of it.

Grabbing my water bottle, I take a swig before the whistle blows. Hopping over the boards, I'm ready to get back out on the ice.

"You ready?" Noah elbows me from where he's standing on the ice.

"Why wouldn't I be?"

He throws his gloved fists up in defense. "Hey, don't come after me. I'm not giving you shit about it."

"Sorry. They're just getting in my head."

"We've got this," he says. "We'll bring it home."

Glancing up at the scoreboard, I know we're doing fine. We're beating Minnesota 5-3 and it's late in the third.

"Damn right, we will."

Our center goes to take the face-off and immediately wins the puck. He sends it to me, and I head down the ice, pushing all earlier thoughts out of my head. Our winger is with me and I shoot the puck his way. He's one of the newer guys on the team, but watching him play is a thing of beauty.

I wonder if that's what I looked like playing at his age. Pretty sure I was playing hockey before he was born, but that's not something I need to get into right now. He's showing off his puck handling skills and before I know it, the puck is in the back of the net.

"Hell, yeah!" I clap him on the helmet, celebrating his goal.

"Nice pass, Jasper," Noah says.

The fans are ecstatic as we extend our lead. Music blares throughout the arena. With only three minutes left and a solid lead, Coach Andrews keeps our line in.

The music stops when the puck drops. For a quick couple of seconds, I watch the guys play before I join the fray because it's hard not to admire their skills.

I used to be that good. Keywords used to be.

I know I don't have much more in me. Between getting old and the fans heckling me more often than not, I'm kind of over this shit.

But I can't hang up my helmet yet. Not when I don't have anything to show for it. I've played with Nashville since I was drafted. Hell, I've been in the league for about twenty years, having been drafted when I was nineteen.

I love this town and this team, and I want to win it all.

We've started out strong this season, but that doesn't mean anything come postseason.

As my shift ends, I head back to the bench.

"Nice work out there, Hayes." Coach claps me on the helmet.

"Well, it looks like you can play hockey," one of the fans behind me chirps.

"Ignore them," Noah says.

"They make it hard some days."

"Well, you are ninety and still playing hockey," Noah says with a shit-eating grin.

"Really? Fuck you, dude."

As the final horn sounds, we beat Minnesota 6-3. It might not have been my best game ever, but getting the W felt good.

After shaking hands with the other team, we skate back toward the tunnel for postgame interviews.

Something I'm not looking forward to.

I know the local press well, but the national media won't be so kind. My suspicions are confirmed when I stop at the first reporter calling my name.

"Jasper, that was a pretty easy pass you missed earlier tonight. Do you think that contributed to Minnesota scoring?"

One deep breath in, hold for four, and let it out. No need to snap and go off on this guy.

"Our goalie did a good job stopping them, so no, I don't think it contributed to them scoring."

If this guy was watching the game, he would know this. They didn't score for another few minutes.

"Do you think it's contributed to a decrease in ice time this season?"

"I leave those decisions up to the coaching staff. I'll always do what's best for the team."

He clears his throat. "The rest of the team looked good. Do you think you'll be able to carry the momentum going forward?"

I don't miss his dig—*the rest of the team.*

"I hope so. You never know what's going to happen, but we're playing well together and have a lot of great new talent."

"Thanks, Jasper."

No "good game" after that. Seriously, one bad play and it's like I've become persona non grata.

Heading to my locker, I throw my gloves and stick down in a huff.

"Don't let them get to you," Marcus says. "We've all been there."

"Difference is I'm the only one that is constantly asked about it."

Dropping down onto my seat, it feels like my entire body creaks. God, I can't remember the last time I didn't have aches and pains. Usually in the offseason they start to fade, but now they're constant.

It fucking sucks.

"I wouldn't listen to them," Bode says.

"Easy for you to say. You had the game of your life. Four goals? That's badass," I say.

"Yeah, it was pretty badass," he says, a grin spreading across his face. "I don't think I've ever scored that many in a game."

"You haven't," Dax comments.

"How do you know? Are you keeping track of my stats?" Bode asks.

"No," he says. "I had to answer the question about you having the best game of your career."

"Why'd they ask you that?" Bode looks confused by this.

"Beats me." Dax shrugs. "But I answered nicely and gave you a glowing review."

Bode ruffles his hair. "Aww, it's like you do love me."

"Yeah, yeah." He pushes him off. "I'm going to go get cleaned up so I can head out."

"Anyone up for a drink?" I ask.

I know the answer before anyone can respond.

"Sorry, can't tonight. I have to relieve the grandmas," Bode says.

"Chloe is waiting for me," Dax confirms.

"My mom has the girls, so Harper and I are having a date night," Marcus says.

"Yeah, yeah," I whine. "You all are going home to the people you love."

"You know, we could set you up," Bode tells me. "I'm sure Stevie or Harper has friends."

"Yeah, doesn't Chloe have a friend that's single?" Marcus asks.

Dax shakes his head. "Her friend Erica is dating someone."

"Do we really not know anyone?" Marcus whispers to Bode out of the corner of his mouth.

"You know you suck at whispering," I say.

"Well, there's usually a lot more noise and I don't have to worry about being heard."

"I'll be fine. You guys go home."

"Need help getting to the showers, old man?"

I flip him off. "Get out of here."

We all go through our postgame routines and I shuck off the rest of my gear, grab a towel, and hit the showers.

It's hard to think that there are more playing days behind me than ahead of me. The good old days are behind me—or at least what I consider the good old days to be. Having played for Nashville my entire career, there haven't been a lot of good days until recently. With shitty coach after shitty coach, we were always the laughingstock of the league until Coach Andrews came in.

He's helped turn around this team more in the last few years than any coach before him. I'm still holding out to see if we might make another run for the Cup.

To see if *I* have it in me to make another playoff run. I don't know how much longer I can put my body through this, but I'll be trying my damndest.

Because I don't have anything else going for me.

After the water starts to run cold, I head back toward my locker. Only a few people are left. Grabbing my phone, the notification that greets me pulls a rare smile from my face. One that only this person seems to be able to bring out in me now.

CATSRCOOL

I think you need a cat

Chapter Two

QUINN

You think I need a cat?

Why is that?

I feel like you're lonely.

How can you tell I'm lonely by a text
message?

I don't know. Are you?

I mean, some days I think I am.

Is today one of those days?

I think so.

Can I help make it less lonely?

Well, you've already made it less lonely
right now

But back to this whole cat thing

What's there to get back to?

I think you need a cat

Why not a dog?

Well, you said you play hockey

I don't think hockey and a dog would mix

So a cat is a good idea?

Yes. Cats are self-sufficient.

And they can be left alone for long stretches of time without you worrying about them.

So that's your reasoning for getting a cat?

It's that I can leave them alone? Won't they be lonely?

Cats do well on their own

And you wouldn't be lonely.

So you think I am lonely

You just said some days you are

Okay, this whole conversation is getting off topic

Promise me you'll at least think about it

I will

Only because it's you and I know that if I don't say that, you'll keep bugging me

You're right

I will keep bugging you

Only because I worry about you

It's a good thing you're cute

You know, you've never actually seen what I look like

I know

Because for some reason, you still won't go out on a date with me.

I have my reasons.

I know.

Maybe if you get a cat, then we can meet

Well, now I really should get a cat just so we can finally meet

Don't get a cat just so you can see me

I mean, what if you hate the cat?

Well, what if the cat hates me?

How could anyone hate you?

You'd be surprised

But what if you like the cat more than me?

Likely possible

Now I'm revisiting this idea

Think about it

Locking my phone, I stuff it into my oversized tote bag and fidget with the ends of my long, blonde hair. I never had nervous tics before. Having been in the spotlight for as long as I can remember, I've always had a spine of steel.

Lately? It seems that steel is wavering. Like when I'm sitting in my lawyer's office.

Floor-to-ceiling glass windows overlook the Nashville skyline. Pinks and oranges fade to dark blues as night creeps in. One of the perks of being a famous pop star? You can meet after hours so people don't see you coming and going.

This isn't the first time I've been in this office, and it won't be the last. Meeting after meeting with my lawyer and Eric's lawyer has gotten us nowhere. The last thing I want is for this to go to trial and become a public fiasco.

Fishing out a piece of gum from my oversized purse, I pop it into my mouth and take a deep breath.

It's all going to work out.

One of the paralegals, Megan, greets me. "Miss Rose. I apologize for your wait."

"Not a problem."

I heft my bag over my shoulder and follow her back to Rebecca's office. A waterfall feature trickles, the melodic tune echoing around the quiet office.

My lawyer, an older woman with gray hair, is sitting behind her all-glass desk when I enter. In a neat pin-striped suit, she's not one to mess with.

"Genevieve. Thanks so much for coming in tonight." She stands, thrusting her hand out to me.

Her corner office looks out over Broadway. People are spilling out of the hockey arena. I wonder when Jasper will head home.

The Knights had an early afternoon game that I watched the beginning of before coming to my meeting.

He didn't look his best last week, but from what I could tell, he cleaned it up today. The thought of talking to him tonight is the only thing getting me through this meeting right now.

"I appreciate you meeting with me after hours."

She grins back at me. "For my biggest client? Anything."

I'm her biggest client?

Considering the fact we're fighting to get the money owed to me, I don't know about that.

"I wish I had better news for you," she says, waving a hand toward one of the black leather chairs.

"Do you have any updates?"

She nods, a grim look washing over her hard features. "Unfortunately, the employee who works for the label has decided not to testify."

"What? Why not?" It bursts out of me before I can stop it. "He's probably using *my* money to pay for some high-powered attorney to intimidate his employees into not speaking out."

She holds her hands up, trying to quiet me. "He's worried about his job. You know how hard it can be to find a job in the music industry."

This time, instead of picking at the ends of my hair, I twiddle my thumbs. "He was our best witness."

"We'll issue a subpoena to compel him to come to court and testify. We're not out of options."

"And if he decides not to testify and be held in contempt?" I lean back in the chair, crossing one leg over the other.

"I've got my paralegals working on other options here. We're combing through Eric's bank records now."

I snort. "I'm surprised he gave those up."

"Like I said, I think they'll lead us to where the money is."

"This is so damn frustrating." I shove a hand through my hair.

"I know. I was hoping for better news, but at the very least, it looks like we have a court date set for the end of February."

That snaps my spine straight. "February? Really?"

Rebecca nods as the paralegal in the corner takes notes of our meeting. "With depositions finished and no settlement offer being accepted—"

"Heaven forbid I ask for what I earned," I interrupt.

"I think," Rebecca continues, "we have a fair judge, so I think it could work out in our favor."

"Really?"

For the first time in months—hell, years—there's a glimmer of hope.

"Yes. I don't want you to get your hopes up, but I think she'll give us a fair and impartial trial."

Even though I didn't want to go to court, if it means putting this whole debacle behind me, I'll do it.

"I'd stop singing today if it meant Eric didn't get another dime from me."

"He knew what he was doing," Rebecca says, shifting a large file on her desk. I know it's mine because it keeps growing every time I come. "I don't think it'll come to you not singing anymore."

"Just starting over with a brand-new label and manager and no money to my name."

"You really think you'd be starting from scratch?" Rebecca asks, a hint of annoyance in her tone.

"Recording a new album takes time and money—"

"And a label that would be willing to invest in you," she

clarifies. "Even though Eric has been skimming off the top from you for years, you're still one of the biggest names in pop music."

"I hate that I was so taken," I confess.

"He is twelve years older than you. He knew exactly what to say to get you to sign that contract without thinking twice."

Back when I was eighteen and first met Eric, he said all the right things. I didn't look twice at my contract. Hell, getting a contract was the most exciting thing to ever happen to me.

When the fame and success started coming in, the money…wasn't there. Eric fed me every line to tell me why I was only making pennies.

Travel expenses.

Recording time in the studio.

Marketing costs.

Considering he was one of the youngest music producers at the time, I believed him. Every artist he signed turned to gold.

It wasn't until I was in the hospital, dehydrated last year from running myself into the ground for him and his label, that I started looking into it.

That's when everything began to fall apart.

"Look, Genevieve, we're doing everything we can to make sure that you get what is yours. I won't stop until you get every penny."

All I can muster is a weak smile. "Thanks, Rebecca."

"Look, go home and relax. Have a glass of wine and try not to worry too much about this, okay?" She drops a warm hand on my shoulder.

"Okay." I stand, slinging my black snakeskin leather tote over my shoulder.

It was the one impulse buy I allowed myself when I

signed my contract. Something I still use to this day. Even though I was suckered into a contract by a man with a charming smile, *my* music and *my* voice earned me this.

I can't change the past, but now? All these years later, I'm fighting for my career.

Fighting for what's mine. Fighting to not be a footnote in a scandal. Fighting to take back the stage.

For me and no one else.

As I head back down the elevator toward the parking garage, I think all the good thoughts that the judge will rule in my favor.

And maybe, just maybe, I'll talk to Jasper tonight.

After all, talking to him makes everything better.

Chapter Three

JASPER

CATSRCOOL

Wish me luck!

THEFRIENDLYGHOST

Good luck!

What am I wishing you luck for?

I have a big work thing coming up

Normally, I'm pretty calm about these things

But this time, I'm nervous

Why are you nervous?

I just want to do this project justice

If you weren't nervous, I think I'd be more concerned

That's oddly comforting

Glad I can help

Between you and my cat, I think I'll be able to make it through

Well, I'll be thinking of you and hoping it all goes well

Thanks

Will you let me know how it goes?

Of course

Pocketing my phone, I grab my coffee and bag, then head into the rink. Weekend afternoon games are my favorite. An easy morning followed by an early night.

The kind where I can soak my aches and pains in peace.

After a conversation with Quinn, I feel even more at ease. Things are normal with her after a weird few weeks. Will the two of us ever meet? I have no clue.

But given that I like talking to her too much, I don't want to push the issue.

"Hey, man." Noah holds the door open for me as I follow Graham inside.

"Hey, guys."

"You look like you're feeling better," Noah says.

I shrug a shoulder, sipping my black coffee. No sugar, no cream. I don't need it to be fancy.

"Not going to let the fans get to me," I say. At least, that's what I keep telling myself.

"That's the spirit," Noah says.

"If it makes you feel better, we don't believe what they're saying," Graham reiterates.

"It just feels like I'm having more bad days than good."

"So is Noah, if it makes you feel better," Graham says.

"Hey!" Noah exclaims. "That was rude."

"What? You said it last night. Only repeating what you said."

I roll my eyes at them. "So I'm down with Noah. Awesome."

He flips me off before pushing open the door to the locker room. My home away from home.

"Nothing wrong with being where we are. We're still on the team."

I waggle my head back and forth. "Is that what counts as pillow talk for you two? Because if so, you suck at it."

"That is—"

Noah can't finish his sentence before Graham is slapping his hand over his mouth. "Please don't tell him anything more. He doesn't need to know."

"And let him think we lie in bed at night discussing what line we're on?" Noah looks horrified.

"I don't really think he needs to know what we discussed last night."

A sly grin washes over Noah's face as he throws an arm around his boyfriend. "No, I don't think he does."

"What are you guys discussing?" Bode asks as we each take our spots in front of our lockers.

"Pillow talk," I deadpan.

Bode shakes his head, rolling his eyes. "I'm sorry I asked…the things we discuss."

"Or don't discuss," Graham clarifies.

I push the guys and their conversation out of my head. I need this time to get into the right headspace for the game. For once, I feel good. The dull aches and pains are still there, but not nearly as present as usual.

We go through the normal pregame routine—warm-ups, music blasting through the locker room, and the usual speech from Coach Andrews.

Marcus leads us all out of the locker room before the game starts. The arena is rocking this afternoon.

Walking to the end of the tunnel, I stop right in front of two women, one of whom is wearing my jersey. And it's not just anybody.

It's Genevieve. The world's biggest pop star. Even though I don't listen to her, I'd have to live under a rock not to know who she is.

Her face is plastered over every billboard up and down Broadway. Every wannabe pop star belts her tunes from the bars.

I've never let myself pay this close attention to her. But as we're waiting to be announced, I can't help but smile at her. Her long blonde hair is curled. Her lips are painted a bright red. Black jeans cling to her curvy hips and thighs.

The jersey she's wearing? That belongs to me.

Damn, does it ever look good.

"You ready for the game?" she asks. Her voice is deep and warm, like a smooth whiskey going down.

"Why are you asking?" I cross my arms over my chest as I eye her. She's a good head shorter than I am in my skates.

She smiles back, a sparkling white smile. "Just making conversation."

"Are you ready to sing?"

"Why are you asking?"

I match her smile. "I don't know. Just making conversation."

"Were you afraid I was going to ask if you're ready after the game last week?"

"God, don't tell me you're going to heckle me about that," I groan.

"You bounced back," Genevieve says. "You looked good last night. No commentary from me."

"For real?"

She nods. "I don't play hockey. I don't think you should take advice from me."

"Just like you probably shouldn't take singing advice from me."

She taps a finger to her temple. "You're pretty smart, Jasper Hayes."

"I can say the same about you, Genevieve. Wearing my jersey? I like it."

It looks really fucking good, but I don't need to tell her that. Hell, I didn't even introduce myself to her, but she knew who I was too.

And I really, really fucking like how my name sounds on her lips.

"I thought it was better than, say, an Evans or Fletcher jersey."

"Damn. Don't let them hear you say that."

"Nah." The corners of her mouth pull into a bigger smile. "I have my favorite player."

"Wow. I'm your favorite? You have good taste. I feel the need to impress you now."

She shakes her head. "You've already impressed me by lacing up your skates tonight. I could never skate."

"I bet you could if you tried."

"Is this an offer to give me lessons?" Genevieve takes a step toward me. Even with the smell of the rink and gear around me, I get a whiff of her perfume.

Something floral and sweet.

"If I had the time between my own skating and you singing."

"Maybe in another life."

I smile down at her as the lights in the rink go dark. I

wish I could continue this conversation with her, but in about thirty seconds, I'll be skating on the ice to the roar of the crowd.

Something about talking to her feels familiar. Easy. It's like I'm not talking to a pop star, and she doesn't seem to see me just as a hockey star.

"I guess that's your cue," she says.

"It is. It was nice to meet you, Genevieve."

"Likewise, Jasper."

I wink at her as I take a step back. "Good luck. Don't mess up the national anthem."

She holds up crossed fingers to me. "Then I should say thanks and good luck to you. Don't mess up your passing."

There's that niggling feeling again. That feeling that something about her is familiar. Maybe it's because I see her face on all those billboards. Our rink is close to downtown, so I see her all the time driving in and out.

That has to be it.

"Thanks." I nod to her as one of the guys calls out to me. "Got to go."

Her eyes widen a fraction of an inch before she waves at me.

Every thought of Genevieve goes out of my mind.

It's game time.

Chapter Four

Holy shit. I just had a conversation with Jasper Hayes.
No, not Jasper Hayes.

The Friendly Ghost Jasper. My Jasper.

The guy I've been messaging with for months. The one that I can't bring myself to meet because…because why?

All the reasons seem meaningless now that we've met in person. Not that he had any clue who I was aside from Genevieve, the pop star. But he didn't treat me like that. He treated me like a normal person.

Something I miss more than I know.

And seeing him in person?

Wow.

I don't think I've ever seen a man so sexy. That chiseled jaw covered in scruff. His dark eyes focused on me. Jasper looks like he could pick me up with one hand and hold me against the wall with ease.

Something not just any person could do with my plus-size curves—ones I'm proud of and will flaunt any chance I can.

"Damn." Claire whistles from beside me. "That was hot."

"What?" I shake myself out of my stupor.

My best friend, Claire, is standing right beside me, jaw nearly on the ground.

"You. Him. Hot."

"*Him* has a name. And it's Jasper."

She grins at me. "Of course you know it."

I look down at my jersey. "I'm wearing his number. Of course I know who he is."

"And I haven't seen you that happy to talk to someone in a long time," she says.

"Excuse me, ladies," one of the team attendants interrupts us. "We're ready for you, Miss Rose."

"Are you nervous?" Claire asks.

I swat at her. "Would you stop asking me that? You know I don't get nervous before things like this."

"Yeah, but you've never sung the national anthem."

I adjust the jersey I'm wearing and roll my eyes at her. "It's just like any other event."

Except this time I'm performing in front of Jasper. And I want to do well for him.

"Ladies and gentlemen. Give it up for one of Nashville's hottest pop stars!" The crowd roars in response. "Here to sing the National Anthem, please welcome Genevieve!"

Taking the microphone from the team attendant, I walk out on the red carpet—one of the Knights' colors—and look around at the sell-out crowd. With one last deep breath, I push every thought from my mind and start singing.

I put my everything into the anthem. It doesn't need anything fancy or to be over-the-top. I belt it out, singing each note to perfection. When I come to the last note, elongating it ever so slightly, the crowd is cheering with enthusiasm.

Before I leave the ice, my eyes scan over the bench, locking on Jasper. His brow is furrowed. *Huh.* I wonder what that's about.

"You crushed it!" Claire greets me with open arms as I come off the ice. "I had chills."

"Thanks. That was fun."

"You should try and do it for the Knights more often."

"Okay." I laugh. "Let's not get ahead of ourselves."

"That was wonderful, Miss Rose." The same woman from earlier comes back over to me and takes the mic from my hand. "If you'd like, I can show you to your suite now."

"Yes, please," Claire answers before I can.

Linking my arm with hers, we take the elevator up a few floors before we're led to a suite.

With the game already started, everyone is in the seats beyond the glass divider. Trays of food and tubs of drinks are laid out in front of us. Grabbing a beer, I crack it open and find two empty seats in the back row.

If there's one thing I don't like missing, it's a Knights game. I've always loved hockey. Before my parents passed away, I would always watch the games with my dad. He was a huge fan. He'd love how they're playing now. Ever since Coach Andrews came on board, they get closer and closer to winning it all.

Will this *finally* be our year?

I hope so.

"Why have you never brought me to a hockey game before?" Claire asks. "It's like a boy aquarium in here."

I choke on my beer. "I'm sorry, what?"

"They're all just down there skating and looking hot doing it."

"And this is why I've never brought you to a hockey game." I shake my head.

"Maybe I'll bring Matt for our anniversary. I think he'd like this too."

"Are you going to call it a boy aquarium to him?" I quirk a brow at her before shifting my attention back to the game.

"He'll get a kick out of it."

"I'm sure."

While everyone is focused on the ice, my gaze flits back to the bench.

Sure, Claire might have a point about how good-looking all the guys are, but I only have eyes for one hockey player.

Jasper.

He's talking with Noah, hand pointing toward the action on the ice. It's sexy to watch him as he surveys the game. Having watched the team for years, it's been easy to see how his passion for the game has floundered as of late.

Tonight? Tonight he looked excited. When he hops off the bench and goes over the boards, I'm ready to watch him play.

"You're giving validity to my boy aquarium with how hard you're staring at all of them."

Her voice startles me out of my thoughts. "I'm only paying attention to the game."

"Sure you are."

She pats my arm and pulls out her phone to start scrolling. I've lost her. Even the "boy aquarium" can't hold her attention for that long. And before I know it, she's heading back into the suite to grab some snacks, bringing a plate for each of us.

Noah and Jasper are working together in perfect sync,

passing the puck back and forth to each other. It's a thing of beauty.

Jasper shoots the puck back to Noah who sends it to him and—

"He scored!" Claire jumps up beside me as the entire arena erupts.

"Hell, yeah!" I high-five her. Jasper's goal? Fucking perfect—hitting the cross bar and going in. A bar down goal. Something he used to be known for when he first came into the league.

Goals for him aren't as common as they once were, but I still love getting to see him play.

Jasper heads back to the bench as play resumes. It's more of the same. The Knights are dominating the game over Florida. Marcus and Bode are the clear stars— expertly moving the puck down the ice and scoring another two goals before putting the game away.

"Tonight was fun," Claire says, wrapping me in a hug, waiting as fans filter out of the arena before leaving. "It was good for you."

I sigh. "It felt normal."

"And you had fun with a guy."

"One that I'll probably never see again."

"So you think."

I don't know why I haven't told my best friend about him. I know exactly who *TheFriendlyGhost* is. She's been pushing me to get out there ever since Eric broke my heart.

Things were good with him at the start, then every-thing changed once I made it big. How can I trust my judgment now?

Do I think Jasper is going to do the same to me as Eric did? No. But it doesn't change my nerves. It's why I keep pushing off meeting him.

"Maybe you don't see him again. But you know, you're allowed to move on from Eric."

I twist a lock of hair around my finger. "It feels like I can't because I'm still stuck in this limbo with him and what I'm owed."

Not to mention that I still have a handful of appearances that I'm contractually obligated to fulfill. Considering we're going to court over contracts, I don't want to give him any more ammunition to use against me by not showing up.

It'll only make me look bad in the end.

"Well, I say once this whole mess is behind you, you reach out to whoever you know with the team and get Jasper's number. I bet he'd be interested. Or finally get on a dating app."

I snort with laughter. "What should I put in my profile then? Down on her luck pop star that might be DTF?"

Claire laughs as we step out into the darkening evening. "I wouldn't go that far. Maybe DTT?"

"DTT?"

"Down to talk." She says this like it's the most obvious thing.

"Well, you go home to your husband, and I'll say I'm DTT then."

"Don't dismiss my idea. It's a good one." Claire hugs me. "Text me when you get home. And give Dolly a kiss for me."

"I should be offended you like my cat more than me."

"Dolly is the best. She loves her Auntie Claire."

"I'll see you later. Bye, babe." I blow her a kiss and head to my car.

When I make it to the safety of my car, I fish my phone out of my bag, a smile coming on immediately.

THEFRIENDLYGHOST

How was your thing tonight?

CATSRCOOL

It went great

I knew it would

How could it not?

I could be leading you on

I could be terrible at my job

There's no way you could be

What about you? Are you terrible at hockey?

I don't think so

Others might disagree

RUDE

But some could say the same about me

Seems I really do need to ruffle some feathers on your behalf

Me too

Need me to fight the bullies on your behalf?

Nah

I can take it

Okay

I don't know if I can throw a punch or not

After bowling, I'm taking you boxing

Throw in some beers, and we've got all the b's covered for our first date

Just name the time and place and I'm there

Mars, seven, tomorrow night

I might be a bit late

My flying skills haven't kicked in yet

Shame

Here I was ready to go

Maybe we can keep it to our planet instead...

Maybe...

If your plans keep you down here, let me know

Chapter Five

JASPER

"**W**hy did you send us a cryptic text to meet you here this morning?"

Noah hops out of his car, zipping up his jacket.

"You were the only ones to respond," I say.

"Where exactly is here?" Graham asks, cup of coffee in hand.

"The Nashville Humane Society."

"Humane Society?" Noah looks confused. "Are we volunteering? Did I miss something?"

He takes the cup of coffee from Graham and sips on it.

"Nope. I'm adopting a cat today."

Both of them stare at me, unblinking.

"You? Adopt a cat?" Noah says before bursting out into laughter.

"Why's that funny?"

"I think what Noah means is that you don't seem like a cat person," Graham says.

"Or an animal person in general." Noah laughs, wiping a fake tear away.

"Fuck off." I flip him the bird. "I'm an animal person."

Well, considering I've only ever owned a goldfish, I don't actually know. But we'll see. Once Quinn floated the idea, I couldn't shake it.

"What if cats aren't a Jasper person?" Noah asks, still laughing.

"How do you put up with him?" I ask Graham, ignoring his boyfriend.

"Do you really want to know?" He grins.

"No."

Opening the door, I walk inside first and spot a young woman sitting behind the desk. "Hi there. Can I help you?"

"Hi there." I flash her a charming smile. "I filled out an online application this week to adopt a cat and made an appointment to meet some you might have available."

"Yes. I'd be happy to assist you. I'm Ashley." She beams back at me. "Your name, please?"

"Jasper Hayes."

She doesn't bat an eye at my name. Either she doesn't watch hockey, or she's much cooler than the average person when meeting an NHL player.

"Ahh, here you are. It looks like you did a virtual home visit with our coordinator and everything got approved."

"Great."

"Why don't you follow me and I'll take you to our meet and greet room. Were you interested in seeing any specific cats?"

"Zucchini," I tell her.

"Perfect. She's a sweetheart. I'm surprised she hasn't been snatched up yet," Ashley says.

"Wow. You've really thought this through," Noah says, as we follow her behind the desk and down a long, cement hallway. "I didn't realize you already got approved."

"I didn't want to say anything in case I was rejected."

"Why would you be rejected?" Graham asks. "You're a hockey player. You have the means to adopt a cat."

"But what if they didn't like my schedule? It's not exactly the easiest to have a pet."

"Hence why we don't have a dog," Graham says.

"Yet," Noah points out.

"You can wait in here and I'll go get Zucchini for you. You can take as long as you want. We want to make sure it's a good fit before you take her home."

"Thanks." I smile at Ashley before she walks out the door.

"She was checking you out," Noah says.

"What?" I whip around to look at him. "No, she wasn't."

"She totally was," Graham confirms. "A stud like you wanting to take home a cat? That's like…well, catnip."

"Please. I don't need anyone," I clarify.

"Aren't you getting a cat because you're lonely?" Graham asks.

"Did I say that?" I cross my arms, glaring at the two of them. "No one said I was lonely."

Except I know I am. With every single one of my teammates pairing off and finding their someones, I go home. By myself.

It's just me. My parents died about ten years ago, and now I'm alone in the world.

If a cat and a woman on the phone is all I have, so be it.

"Here is Zucchini," Ashley says, walking back into the room. "Take your time. If you need me, I'll be out at the desk."

"Thank you."

The small, grayish brown cat sits on its hind legs, staring me down. It's like being out on the ice and staring down an opponent. Except this one is studying me more than any defender would.

"Hey, sweet girl."

I hold the back of my hand out to her to sniff.

"Her name is Zucchini?" Noah laughs.

"What's wrong with that?" I ask as she comes closer. She licks the back of my fingers before burrowing into my hand.

It's the cutest fucking thing ever.

"Why not Carrot or Onion?" Noah asks. "I mean, is she a Zucchini?"

"Are you a Noah?" I fire back.

"Ouch." Graham looks between us as I drop down onto my ass for Zucchini to come closer.

A few toys are strewn about the room and I grab one to entice her closer. According to her profile online, Zucchini likes playing with toys, snuggling, and curling up in your lap to sleep.

Grabbing one of the teaser toys, I hold it out to her as she paws it. She swats at it immediately. It's the cutest fucking thing I've ever seen as she rolls onto her back to play with it.

"She likes me."

"You or the toy?" Noah fires back.

"Do you have to be such a dick?" Graham asks before I can.

"I'm just making sure that you like her. I mean, it's a big commitment. She's the only one that would suffer if you decide you don't like her."

The cat in question swats the toy away before settling onto her haunches and staring me down. It's like she's trying to decide whether she can trust me or not.

There wasn't much online about why she's here, but I

was drawn in by her sweet face. Those big brown eyes staring me down.

You can trust me. I convey it with my eyes. As if she can read my mind, she steps into my lap and curls up before licking her paw.

"What a good Zucchini."

"Seriously, Zucchini, really?" Noah snorts. "I can't believe someone named her that."

It's like the cat senses his bitterness when he drops down to try and say hi. She hisses at him immediately.

"She apparently has good taste in men because she doesn't like you."

"Hey. It's not my fault the cat is a twatopotamus."

She moves away from me and closer toward Noah, sniffing his outstretched hand.

"Well, apparently she doesn't mind it when I call her that."

The tiny ball of fur burrows into his hand.

"If you gave my cat a dumb nickname…"

Noah smiles at her, ignoring me. "Maybe we should adopt a cat, Graham."

"Do you want a cat? I thought we were dog people," he asks.

"You don't have a dog," I clarify, scratching Zucchini behind the ears, who hasn't moved far. Apparently she is a daddy's girl.

"Well, maybe it's because we need a cat instead," Noah points out.

"Who's going to watch this hypothetical cat?"

I'm not looking at them as I lift Zucchini back into my arms. She curls up as I continue petting her. I can't help but think of telling Quinn about this.

Sure, it might have been her suggestion, but really, after hanging out with this girl for a few minutes, I see the appeal. Graham and Noah are arguing about if they should get a cat or dog and I tune them out.

They have each other.

Me? I have someone on the other end of a phone that is too nervous to meet, yet has convinced me I'm lonely and need a cat.

Who knew someone I've never met could be right about me?

I needed a fucking cat.

"So, what do you think?" Ashley asks, coming back into the room.

"I'll take her."

"That's wonderful. I'll get a copy of the adoption contract, and since you were already approved, you can take her home today if you're ready." Her eyes fill with gratitude and excitement.

"I have a carrier in my car. I'm all set."

"Even better."

"I think we know what Jasper will be like as a dad," Noah says.

"Better than you two." I smile as Zucchini licks my hand again. Seriously, how have I not gotten a cat before now? This is the cutest thing ever.

"Twatopotamus is going to have you wrapped around her little finger," Noah tells me.

"Paw," I correct. "And if *Zucchini* wants something, she'll get it."

"Yup, he's going to be the biggest sucker of a dad," Graham confirms.

I ignore them as I coo all over this cat in my arms as she fawns over me. In a matter of minutes, we have a bond. I will do anything to protect her, even if it means letting Noah call her that dumbass name so she'll snuggle up to him.

Because I'm taking this cat home and I only hope the guys like her like I do. She's not going anywhere. Maybe it'll finally get Quinn to meet me. Not that I'm getting Zucchini for her, but fuck, if it lets me finally meet her, I'll take it.

I'll take whatever I can get with Quinn because I'm hooked.

And while I won't tell the guys that, I know I am.

Whatever she gives me, I'll take until the day we meet. Because she is worth it.

Chapter Six

JASPER

It's the breed

That's a good one

That's what they told me at the shelter

You know, when I told you to get a cat, I didn't mean you had to go out and get the first cat you see

She was sitting there looking so cute

It was impossible to say no to her

<<picture of cat curled up on lap looking at camera>>

I think she looks even cuter sitting with you

What's her name?

Zucchini.

Or as Noah likes to call her, Twatopotamus

Twatopotamus

I'm sorry, what?

She hissed at Noah when they first met

He called her that and then she warmed up to him

I'm hoping the name won't stick

Send me another picture of Zucchini

<<picture of Zucchini sleeping>>

Is she purring and having little cat dreams?

Yes

Dreams about what? I don't know

Probably dreaming of all the toys that
you're going to give her because you're
going to be such a pushover

Going to be?

I already bought half the pet store for her

Yep, I knew it

You're a total pushover

What do you say you come over and
meet her?

See what a real pushover I am

You want me to come over and meet her?

Well, and meet me too

Added side benefit

I don't know

How long are we going to chat on this thing
before we take it to real life?

I don't know

I was thinking at least a solid year

Might as well make it two years then

Don't give me any ideas

I'm serious

I want to meet you, Quinn

Would you really say no to Zucchini?

I mean, that face is very hard to say no to

I mean, I can barely say no to my cat and
I've had her for two years now

So…is that a yes?

Can I think about it?

I'm not sure what there is to think about

Either you want to meet or you don't

But if you need time, take it

Yes

To what?

To meeting

Wait, really?

Yes.

I thought I'd have to send more pictures of
Zucchini to get you to say yes

You can take more time if you need it

If I say maybe again, will you send more
pictures of Zucchini?

<<picture of Zucchini licking paw>>

Okay. Zucchini is the cutest damn thing
ever and I'm only coming over so I can
meet her

I'll take what I can get

When do you want me to come over?

Free Sunday afternoon?

I can be

I'll text you my address

See you around three?

It's a date

I'm pacing. I've never been a pacer. Zucchini is sitting on her cat throne, staring out the window without a care in the world. It's her favorite place to be—looking down on Broadway high up from my condo.

Every so often, she glances over at me to make sure I'm still here. We're still feeling each other out. From what I can tell, she likes me. She loves lying next to me or on my lap. Having her here when I get home is nice. Even if she doesn't greet me half the time, knowing I'm not alone is comforting.

I glance at the clock on the oven. It's three now.

"She should be here soon, Zucchini."

All I get in response is a meow.

"Why am I talking to a cat? It's not like you know what I'm saying."

For all I know she's thinking about what's for dinner or where she's going to sleep tonight.

I'd like that life. Not a care in the world.

Instead, I'm sitting here watching the clock hands move farther and farther away from three with no sign of Quinn.

Three ten.

Three fifteen.

Nothing.

Well, fuck. This isn't good. I scrub a hand down my

face and grab a beer from the fridge. Too early for the hard stuff.

Taking a deep breath, I crack it open and let the icy cold liquid slide down my throat.

I thought I finally made progress. That we were going to meet and that'd be it. That we would have gotten past her nerves of *finally* meeting.

I guess not.

I hope I didn't screw this up before it even started.

Pulling up the Music City Matches app, I fire off a message to her.

THEFRIENDLYGHOST

Are you still coming?

Did you get lost?

Are you okay?

NOTHING. No response.

What if something did happen?

THEFRIENDLYGHOST

Are you there?

I'm worried something's happened to you

Will you at least let me know you're okay?

THREE THIRTY COMES and goes before my phone finally buzzes from where it's sitting on the counter.

Thank fuck.

CATSRCOOL

I'm sorry

I thought I could do it but I can't

THEFRIENDLYGHOST

I don't know what to say…

I STALK toward the living room and drop onto the sofa. Anything I say right now would come off as angry. Because I am. I don't want to be, not with Quinn, but fuck. I don't know what it's going to take to meet this woman in person.

We've been talking for months. That's a full-blown relationship at this point. We've never even exchanged phone numbers.

THEFRIENDLYGHOST

It feels like I did something

CATSRCOOL

It's not you

So it really is me then?

No!

I told you I got my heart broken before

And…

> I get that, I do

> But you're not even giving this a chance

What if we meet in person and we have
absolutely zero chemistry?

> Well, we'll never know unless we meet

But I don't want to lose what we have now

> Like I said, you have to take a chance on us

> And if you're not going to take a chance…

What are you saying?

WHAT AM I SAYING? Do I want to keep this thing going
over the phone for another year? Two years? What if
Quinn is never ready to meet and I'm just stuck waiting for
her? I don't want that.

Zucchini comes and curls into my side. Clearly she
knows what I need right now. It helps make up my mind. I
take a pic and send it to Quinn.

> When you decide you're ready to meet us,
> we'll be here

> But until then, I can't keep doing this

Jasper, please

> Figure out what you want, Quinn

> Because I know what I want

I want us to give this thing a chance

A real chance

Take your time, Quinn

It's obvious you need it

I'll be here when you're ready to meet

MY HEART TWISTS as I close out of the app. There is nothing I want more than to meet Quinn. To keep talking with her. Confessing things I like and don't like. What movies I'm watching.

But I can't.

I want more. I want what my teammates have. If Quinn ever gives us a chance, we could have it.

Until she's ready, I'll wait.

Even if it might kill me.

Chapter Seven

JASPER

"Okay, how the fuck do I tie a bow tie?" I ask, fidgeting with the damn material around my neck. Not for the first time tonight.

"How have you never tied a bow tie before?" Noah asks, swatting my hand away. Using deft fingers, he ties it with ease.

"Excuse me. I always did the clip-on ones."

"That says a lot," Noah snickers.

"Fuck off." I grab my drink from the table and take a sip. "And thank you."

Having done fancy events in the past, I should be able to manage to tie a scrap of fabric together, but I can't.

Maybe if I had someone like Quinn to help me.

Fuck. I should not let my thoughts stray there. No good will come of it.

"Look, you need to put on a happy face for a few hours and then you can be done," Marcus says.

"Who says I'm not happy about tonight?"

He waves a hand in my direction. "Whatever you're thinking right now gave you a look."

Bode nods his head in agreement. "The kind that says you're mad about something."

"I'm fine." It's little more than a growl, but at this point, I don't care.

It's been almost a week since I last talked to Quinn. It's the longest we've gone since we started talking. Well, except for the time she ghosted me, but she had her reasons.

This is more self-inflicted.

Because I can't keep falling for her if she's never going to want to meet in person. I couldn't take it. Hell, I'm already halfway in love with her.

"We're going to go upstairs and grab the girls. Want to meet us in the ballroom?" Bode asks.

"Sure."

We all leave Marcus's room, and while the guys head upstairs to their partners, Noah, Graham, and I head toward the ballroom. We spent the afternoon bowling before heading to the hotel to get ready for the evening ahead.

We haven't even made it into the ballroom, and everything about this hotel is grand. Velvet curtains hang from the walls with low, flickering lights. Waiters with trays of champagne greet us. It's bougie as fuck, and the team wants us to wine and dine everyone to get them to open their pocketbooks to raise money for the team's new charity this year.

"Wow." I let out a low whistle as we enter the ballroom.

Tall vases of flowers sit on each table surrounded by small, flickering candles. Long swaths of white fabric hang from the walls and ceiling with glittering lights behind them. People are milling about as servers in white jackets serve hors d'oeuvres and glasses of champagne.

I grab a glass and take a gulp.

"You sure you're okay?" Graham asks, eyeing me over his own glass.

Some of our teammates are already here, lingering near the walls so as not to be the first to break the ice.

"Would you guys quit asking me that? I'm fine."

"Sure you are," Noah says. "Maybe you just miss Twatopotamus."

"Her name is Zucchini," I growl. "That is not catching on."

"Oh yeah, he misses his cat." Noah ignores me. "That's pretty cute."

Ignoring them, I find our table and drop down into my chair. All of the guys and their partners come and take their seats.

This is one of those times I hate being the only single person. The empty seat next to me is a glaring reminder that I'm alone.

Who knows? If Quinn had decided to come over and meet Zucchini—and me—maybe she'd be here with me tonight.

I make idle chitchat with everyone, eating my bland chicken.

It's fine. It's like every other fundraising gala before this one. I've never brought anyone before, so why am I moping about it now?

Maybe it's because I wish I had someone with me? I can't imagine what would have happened if I told the guys about Quinn and wanting to bring her and then she didn't show up.

I don't know if I could ever live down that embarrassment.

Before long, we're shuffled out of our seats after dinner before Genevieve takes the stage. Something I know because the girls have talked about it all night.

She's a force on stage. In a black dress with a cut-out on the side, it highlights her curvy figure.

Hell, maybe I could try and talk to her again. We had fun talking for those few minutes before she sang the national anthem.

Couldn't hurt.

The universe must be working in my favor when she walks in our direction after finishing a few songs.

"Hi there." Genevieve comes up to our table. "I'm Genevieve. It's nice to meet you."

I snort but Bode elbows me in the side.

"What?" I throw my hands up in defense. "It's not like she needs to introduce herself when she's the world's biggest pop star."

She smiles at me and it does funny things to my insides. "It's only polite."

"More polite than him." Bode laughs.

"It's nice to meet you…" Genevieve holds her hand out to me.

"Jasper." Taking her hand, a flash of electricity moves up my arm. "But we've already met before."

Should I be offended she doesn't remember me?

She flashes me an award-winning smile. "I think I'd remember if I'd met one of the Knights' greatest players."

"Then she clearly hasn't met you," Bode jokes.

"Ouch. You going to let him talk to you like that?" Genevieve asks me before turning her attention toward Bode. "I think you should respect your elders."

"He's not that much older," Bode mumbles

"We're meeting the world's biggest pop star and you guys are arguing over who is older?" Harper shakes her head. "I'm sorry, we can't take these guys anywhere."

"They're always like this," Stevie confirms. "But we love them anyway."

"They sound like keepers," Genevieve says.

"That they are," Chloe says, smiling at Dax.

"Well, it was nice to meet you all. I was taking a quick break but need to get back up on stage." She throws up the peace sign. "Got to go."

"Who says that?" Noah laughs as she retreats.

"Holy shit." My eyes fly to the space Genevieve vacated.

"What?" Dax asks.

"It's her."

"Her who?" Marcus asks, looking confused now.

"*Her*," I reiterate.

"Okay, you saying her again doesn't help me know who *her* is," Marcus says.

"I have to go."

I set my drink down on the table and run. Fast. I don't want her getting away. Not when I'm finally in the same room with her.

Busting out of the double doors of the ballroom, I look both ways. A flash of blonde hair turns the corner at the end of the hall and I chase after her.

I am not letting her out of my sight.

"Genevieve!" I shout after her.

The hallway is quieter back here. She's moving fast for being in a pair of tall, silver heels.

"Genevieve." I try again. This time I'm closer. I see her hesitate for a moment before she keeps walking.

Not breaking stride, I call out again.

"Quinn."

She stops dead in her tracks.

Bingo.

Chapter Eight

QUINN

"Quinn."

A shiver racks my body at his voice saying my name. His warm, smoky voice feels like whiskey going down.

Finding an open door to my left, I dart inside. The ballroom is void of people, set up for an event. Pink curtains hang from the walls as tables are set with place settings and flowers.

I should be going back and getting ready to finish my performance, but right now, I need a minute.

The door closes behind me as the air shifts.

A minute I won't be getting.

I can't bring myself to turn around and look at the man that consumes my every thought, not just tonight but for the last few months.

"Quinn?"

This time, it comes out as a question.

Sucking in a deep breath, I try to quell the raging nerves as I turn around. I've never been more nervous in my life.

Not the first time I took the stage. Not the first time I played before a sold-out crowd.

Turning around and looking Jasper in the eyes for the first time—knowing that he knows who I am—has my stomach swooping down near my feet.

Those beautiful brown eyes are staring at me like they know every bit of my soul.

"Quinn."

It's just my name again as he closes the distance between us. Our toes touch. In my heels, I'm almost at eye level with him.

I drink my fill of this sexy man standing before me. In a tux, he looks even more handsome than I thought possible. Jasper in his hockey uniform? Sexy.

In a tux?

I bite my lip to keep my groan from escaping.

It's the biggest turn-on that has my panties going up in flames.

"Jasper."

He smiles, resting a hand on my waist. His thumb brushes over the exposed skin on my side.

"Say it again," he whispers.

"Jasper."

"Fuck, Quinn." His breath ghosts my lips. "Do you know how long I've waited to hear you say my name?"

I smile. "A while, I'm guessing."

Jasper's strong hand cups my cheek. "Yeah. A while."

"And?"

"And what?"

"Are you mad at me?"

"For not telling me who you are?" he asks.

"Yeah."

"I mean, would I have believed you if you said you were Genevieve?"

Grabbing the lapels of his jacket, I tug him close. His hard, muscly chest melds against mine.

"You would've thought I was lying."

"Probably." He nods.

"We had a good thing going. I didn't want to ruin it," I confess.

"Had? Do you think this thing is over?"

"I hope not…" I trail off.

Fire burns hot in Jasper's eyes. It jumps between us, simmering in my veins. One look from this man and I'm a puddle.

The sweet smell of bergamot overwhelms me. It's so Jasper that I'll never be able to smell it and not think of this man.

This strong and sexy man who finally knows who I am.

Jasper brushes a lock of hair out of my face before dropping his lips to my ear. "Are you a cat?"

I burst out laughing. "Are you feline a connection?"

"I think it broke the ice."

"It definitely did."

Jasper stares down at me, his eyes moving all over my face. "It's hard to believe it's you. That you're in my arms. I've dreamt about this."

"Really?" My heart pitter-patters in my chest.

He nods. "I never thought the day was going to happen. I wanted it more than anything."

"Even more than a Stanley Cup?"

His mouth quirks up in a smile. "I mean…"

"I see where I fall in the grand scheme of things."

"If it helps, it's basically a tie."

I wrap my arms around him. "Anything I can do to break the tie?"

"Tell me a bad joke."

"That's what you want?" Laughter laces my voice.

This is what I love about being with Jasper. How easy things are with him.

"It's either that or you force feed me Brussels sprouts. And if yours aren't—"

"Inspired, I believe was the word you used," I cut him off.

"Which is why I went with a joke."

"Fine." I tap my finger against my chin, trying to come up with something on the fly. "What do you call a cat prom?"

"I don't know. What?"

I swat at his chest. "You're not even going to guess?"

"I just want to hear you talk," he says.

"A fur ball."

"That was terrible." He laughs. "You know a lot of cat jokes."

"I figured I'd need them to impress you. And Zucchini."

"You know, she's not going to believe I met you. She might be jealous."

"Your cat is going to be jealous of me?" I ask.

He nods. "Yes. I might have divulged a lot of our relationship to her. She's a very good listener. Not judgmental at all."

"I'm excited to meet her."

He pulls out his phone and passes it over. "Does this mean I can finally get your real number and have you over?"

I smile, punching it in and texting myself. "Yes."

"I feel like I can't stop smiling," Jasper says. "It's weird that tonight of all nights we met."

His hand closes over mine as I pass his phone back. There's that spark again. It's an innocent touch, but charged and full of tension.

It's what has the words escaping my lips before I can stop them.

"I'm so glad you finally know."

His brows furrow.

"Wait, finally? What's that supposed to mean?"

Shit.

Shit, shit, shit. How am I going to get myself out of this?

"Did you know who I was?"

Jasper pulls out of my hold, an arctic chill filling the space.

"Not at first."

"At first? Are you serious?"

I'm fidgeting again, twirling the ends of my hair. Is there any way I can backtrack out of this?

"When you said you played hockey, and then told me your name, it wasn't a leap to put two and two together."

He starts to pace in front of me, a frenetic energy pulsing off him.

"Instead of telling me that you knew who I was, you just led me on."

"No," I say, louder than necessary. "That wasn't it at all."

"So, what? Just seeing if you could bag a hockey player?"

"Jasper," I scoff. "I didn't know it was you at first. But everything I told you was the truth. I never lied."

He stops, resting his hands on his hips. The same hands that were just on me. Ones that I wish were still there.

"Except for the fact that you knew who I was while I was just swinging my dick around not knowing who *you* were."

"Really?" I roll my eyes. "You said it yourself; you wouldn't have believed me if I told you who I was."

"God, I feel so stupid." Jasper pushes a hand through his hair.

"Jasper, please," I beg, grabbing his arm to try and stop him.

That jolts him out of his stupor.

"I can't be here."

Dread slides through my veins like ice. "You're leaving?"

"And here I thought I'd found the real thing."

Jasper is out the door before I can say anything else.

"Shit!" I yell into the empty room.

Before the door can shut, a group of people starts walking in. Not wanting to get sucked into any conversation, I find a side exit to leave.

I still have to finish my performance. How in the world am I supposed to go up on stage and sing about love when all I want to do is find Jasper and apologize to him?

It's not like I was lying. More of a lie by omission.

But really, is it my fault that he gave me just enough to figure out who he was and I played it closer to the vest? Would he have still wanted to talk to me if I told him I knew who he was?

Would he have been that open and honest with me?

Fuck. Everything is a mess.

Meeting Jasper was supposed to be the easy part. It was supposed to be on *our* terms. Not thrown together by coincidence. I thought that acting like I don't remember meeting him at the game might throw him off. Because if I showed how much it meant to me, would he know that CatsRCool was me?

That way, when we finally got to meet—*for real*—he wouldn't be angry.

Way to go, Quinn.

You might have just scared off the most perfect man you've ever met because you were too chicken to meet him in person.

Finding the door to the makeshift stage in the ballroom, I push all these thoughts from my head.

Jasper. His face when he left. The fact that he might never want to talk to me again.

Performance face on.

Because that's what I have to do.

Time for Quinn to take a back seat… Genevieve has a job to do.

Chapter Nine

I *fucked up.*

It's the very first thought that plagues me when I wake up. Not even Dolly purring and wanting snuggles can distract me from how badly I messed up.

Checking my phone proves to be a fruitless effort. No messages. No red numbers signaling a notification. There's no point in texting or messaging him on the app. He doesn't want to hear from me. I've sent him a few messages since the gala.

The only messages I've gotten since are from my lawyer. Nothing new on that front, which doesn't do anything to improve my mood.

Because I keep picturing Jasper as he left.

God, I wish I could get the look on his face out of my mind.

Maybe if we didn't meet so suddenly I could have come up with a plan to tell him I knew who he was.

"Dolly, I really stepped in it."

She purrs against my leg, curling up next to me.

It's a dreary day, rain pattering against the skylights in

my bedroom. I don't have the energy to get up. Thank God for the automatic feeder for Dolly, or she'd be mad at me too.

Glancing at my phone, I realize it's still early. Hoping my friend is awake, I tap her phone number and wait for her to answer.

"Why are you calling me so early? Are you okay?"

"I'm fine, but I need my friend."

"Okay, when you say it like that, I'm worried," Claire whispers.

"Can I tell you something and you not yell at me?"

"Why would I yell at you?" she asks. I can hear the confusion in her voice.

"Because I didn't tell you something and I don't want you to get mad at me. Someone is already mad and I don't know if I can take anyone else being mad at me right now."

"I won't yell."

"Promise?" I ask.

"Promise," Claire confirms.

"I met someone."

"You met someone?" she shrieks over the phone. Based on the groan that filters through the phone, she's in bed still.

"Yes. On a dating app."

"You met someone on a dating app?"

"Not just anyone. Jasper Hayes."

"Why does that name sound familiar?"

"He's the hockey player we met when I did—"

"You met Jasper Hayes on a dating app?!" I hold the phone away, her voice increasing by at least five decibels. "I'm not yelling *at* you. But you met him? The guy I said you should totally get his number?"

"One and the same." I wince.

"Why didn't you tell me?"

"I was scared."

"Scared I'd be mad? Hang on." I wait a beat before my phone buzzes in my ear. She's video calling me.

"Why in the world are you video chatting with me so early?"

I rest the phone against my other pillow and curl up against my own.

"Because this is a conversation we should be having over wine, but it's too early for that. When did this all start?"

"A few weeks after everything went down with Eric."

Claire shakes her head. She knows exactly when this was. "Eric dumps you and you decide to get back out there on a dating app and then you discover that Eric has been stealing from you for years. I mean, why wouldn't you want to tell me you found someone new?"

"It's why I didn't tell anyone," I confess. "It's not like Jasper has access to my bank accounts, but I was still nervous."

"And? How is he?"

"How is he what?"

"In bed!" Claire shrieks again. "If you're calling me this early, I hope it's with details."

"The only details are I figured out who he was and I didn't tell him who I was. And we just so happened to bump into each other again last night at the Knights gala."

"Does he know who you are now?"

I wince again. "He does now."

"Why does that look like a bad thing based off your face?" She rests her phone against the wall and starts making coffee.

"Because he thought I was lying to him by not telling

him I already knew who he was. He was mad, Claire. I couldn't even get a chance to apologize."

"Shit." She drops a pod in her machine and rests on her elbows to look down at me. If only she were here and could make me a cup. I don't even have the energy to call for delivery.

"Yeah. We've been talking for months and he kept wanting to meet, but I was worried."

"Worried he wouldn't believe it was you?"

"Yeah. It's not like I was lying to catfish him or something."

"But it was still a lie of omission," she says.

"Ugh. How am I going to make it up to him?"

"Is he worth it?" Claire asks.

I blink at the camera. Blink again. "Would I be calling your ass this early in the morning if he wasn't?"

"Okay. Fine. Just wanted to make sure."

"We've been talking for months. I know things about him he's probably never told anyone else."

"Like?" she fishes.

"Nope, not telling you." I shake my head.

"Well, maybe one of those things is going to be how you get back into his good graces. Send him an apology. If he won't talk to you, that might get his attention."

"But how would I get it to him when I don't know when he'll be there?"

She rolls her eyes, harder than usual…like to get me to see it on the tiny square camera. "Good thing you know where he works."

I smack myself on the forehead. "Of course. Now I just need to think of something good enough."

Something that shows Jasper I really know him. That I'm sorry and I wasn't leading him on.

"See? This is why you called me. I'm the genius."

"Yeah, yeah. I know."

Her coffee starts streaming down into her cup. "Coffee's ready. I'm going to go wake up the hubster, and in the meantime, text me any ideas you might have to win back Jasper's heart."

"I will."

She shakes her head, sipping from her mug. "I can't believe you let me prattle on about how well you and Jasper would go together and you knew him the whole time."

I point a finger at her. "He didn't know who I was then."

"My point exactly. If you have that much chemistry with someone who didn't even know who you were, then clearly you two are a fit and I called it."

"Can you call it when I was already messaging with him?"

"Let me have this one." She laughs. "And maybe if you go to a game to win him back, you can take me to the boy aquarium with you?"

She waggles her brows at me.

"You said you wouldn't call it that anymore."

"I get one more." She holds up her finger. "Consider it your payment for lying *to me*."

"You said you weren't mad!" I scoff.

"I'll pretend to be if it means I can call it that." She winks.

"I'm hanging up now. Goodbye."

"Love you!"

I tap the screen to end the call. Sitting up, I pull Dolly into my lap and start to scratch behind her ears.

Whatever I do, it has to be good. And include Zucchini.

Which gives me an idea. I only hope it means Jasper will talk to me again.

Chapter Ten

JASPER

It's early. Practice doesn't start for another few hours, but I needed to come in and clear my head. Ever since the gala, I've been spinning out. Finding out that the woman I've been talking to knew who I was this whole time?

It feels like a betrayal. I don't care that she's the world's biggest pop star. I hate that she lied about knowing who I was.

I need to put Quinn out of my head. Or is it Genevieve?

I feel like such an idiot to let myself get played like that.

Throwing my bag into my locker with a little more force than necessary, I stalk off to the weight room.

It's blissfully empty.

Grabbing a set of weights, I start my normal workout routine. Today, the burn is welcome. I need it.

It helps clear my head, pushing away all thoughts of the gala and the woman I've been talking to these last few months.

By the time I got home that night, there were messages

waiting for me from her. I couldn't bring myself to look at them—I was too mad. Still haven't, if I'm being honest, no matter how tempting they are.

Dropping the weights and grabbing a heavier set, I move on to lunges. Until a towel swats me in the ass.

"What the fuck?" I set the dumbbells down, turning to find the guys behind me.

"What's got you in such a mood this morning?" Bode asks.

"Who says I'm in a mood?"

He exchanges a look with Marcus. "Oh yeah, obviously not in a mood."

I wipe the sweat from my brow with the bottom of my T-shirt.

"You've been in a mood since the gala," Bode says.

"Just tired, is all," I lie. "I'm fine."

I am not ready to get into a discussion about this.

"You know, you keep saying you're fine, but I'm finding that hard to believe."

"All I want right now is to focus on my workout and look ahead to playing against Carolina. What's wrong with that?"

"Nothing," Graham says.

"See?" I point at him. "He agrees. Nothing wrong with wanting to keep up with the younger kids so the fans won't give you shit."

"You know you don't have to prove anything to anyone, right?" Dax says.

"I know."

"So then why are you here so early pushing yourself?"

"You're here early," I retort.

"Practice starts in thirty minutes. Not that early," Bode says. "How long have you been here?"

Shit. A lot longer than I thought.

"All I want is to keep my head down and play my game. I know I'm not cutting it like I used to."

It's no surprise that my game isn't up to par as I'm getting older.

"No one said that," Marcus tells me.

"Yeah, but every time I come off the ice and sit on the bench, fans yell at me about how terrible I'm doing."

Marcus scoffs. "Has Coach Andrews said that?"

"Well, no," I bite out.

"Then don't worry about it. You're doing just fine."

"Right."

Except it doesn't feel like I am as I head over to the treadmills and fire one up. There's too much going on in my head right now. I'm pissed that Quinn lied to me. I'm mad that my game isn't up to my usual level. I'm pissy with the fans.

I'm just over it all right now.

Lately, the person who I would talk to about this is Quinn. I told her everything. I mean, I used to be able to talk to the guys about anything, but with all of them falling in love, I don't want to be a burden.

It's the hard part of not having any family. No one that I can turn to and talk to about these kinds of things. It's like I'm being left behind and I don't quite know how to deal with that.

At least I have Zucchini. But she has to like me because I feed her and pet her.

Jabbing at the treadmill button, I increase the speed.

The pounding underneath my feet feels good. The burning and stretching in my legs and lungs keeps driving me forward.

This. This is exactly what I need right now.

Except it comes to an abrupt end when Noah stands in front of me, pulling the safety magnet off.

"What the fuck, man?" I glare at him.

"Tell me what's going on."

Looking around, I see that the other guys left.

"Why does anything have to be wrong? I'm—"

"If you say fine one more time, I'm going to deck you."

"Really? You would punch me?"

"Well, no, not really." He shakes his head. "But everyone knows when someone says they're fine, they're not actually fine."

"Excuse me, Mr. Hayes?" One of the team secretaries walks into the weight room, looking very out of place in her pantsuit.

"Yes." I grab the towel hanging from the bar of the treadmill and drag it down my face, trying to make myself more presentable.

"This came for you."

She thrusts a box into my arms before scurrying out.

"Thanks," I call out, even though the door is closing behind her.

"What's that?" Noah asks.

"Beats the fuck out of me."

Too bad it wasn't Coach Andrews needing me so I could get out of this conversation with Noah.

Grabbing one side of the box, I rip it open. A note addressed to Casper sits on top of two neatly wrapped items in pink tissue paper. I grab the card and open it to an unfamiliar scrawl.

Casper,

I know you don't want to talk to me,

but I'm hoping you might still be feline a
connection and this will break the ice...again.

<3
Bella

"WHO THE FUCK IS CASPER?"

I drop the note into the box, trying to hide it from Noah who's reading over my shoulder.

"Mind your own business."

Setting the package down on one of the benches, I take out one of the items and unwrap it. A box of Frosted Flakes. Another note is taped to the front.

Maybe you can convince me to like
cereal on our first date.

<3
Bella

THAT PULLS a smile to my face. Putting the cereal away, I grab the smaller package and unwrap it. It's a new catnip toy.

Because Zucchini can't be left out <3

. . .

I SNORT A LAUGH. Only Quinn would apologize by remembering to include something for my cat.

"Alright. You're smiling. I think I've seen you do that a whole three times since I joined the team. What is this and what the hell is going on?"

So much for getting out of this conversation. There's no way I can avoid it now.

"If I tell you, will you promise not to tell the guys?" I request, knowing it's probably an impossible ask. I don't know how these guys are so gossipy, but they are.

"As long as you promise to fill them in. You know we only bug you because we care," he says. "But also, you know I'll tell Graham. I can't *not* tell him."

I weigh what he's offering. Telling his boyfriend I get. The two of them tell each other everything. They're disgustingly in love, something I want. Promising to tell the guys? Maybe.

"Can I think about it if I tell you?"

"Deal." A shit-eating grin spreads across his face as he sticks his hand out for me to shake.

"I met someone."

"You did?" His jaw drops and I smack him in the bicep.

"Don't act so surprised."

"I just didn't know you liked…people."

I not so subtly flip him off. "You're making me regret telling you this."

"Sorry. Continue."

He crosses his arms and leans against the mirrored wall.

"Well, I met someone who turned out to be a pop star."

"You don't have to lie." He rolls his eyes.

"I'm serious. It's Quinn. Well, Genevieve."

"Now I know you're lying. You met the world's biggest pop star?"

I nod. "On a dating app. Although, I didn't realize it was her until the other night."

"Wait…" The wheels are turning as he's starting to put everything together. "You said it was *her* the other night. Was that the first time you met?"

"Yup." I pop the *p*. "And it turns out she knew exactly who I was."

"So what's the problem?" Noah asks. "If she knew who you were and likes your grumpy ass, I don't see what the problem is."

"She knew who I was and didn't tell me."

"And?" Noah rolls his hand to tell me to keep going.

"And I had no idea who she was and I'm pissed."

"Pissed that she knew who you were and you didn't know who she was, or pissed that she didn't tell you?"

"Both."

"Well, clearly she's the smarter of you two."

"I'm regretting telling you this at all," I say.

"Then next time don't open packages from mystery people around me. But I think you're in the wrong here, Jasper."

"Really?"

He nods. "Yes. If you like her, what's the problem? I wouldn't tell people who I am if I was as famous as she is. And besides…"

"Besides what?"

"It's not like you told her who you were."

"Fair," I grumble.

"She might not have admitted knowing who you were,

but it seems like she knows you." He points toward the box. "She even got a present for Twatopotamus."

"What have I told you about calling Zucchini that?"

"She likes it."

"No, she doesn't."

"Doesn't matter," Noah says. "What does matter is what you're going to do next. Finding anyone these days is hard. So she didn't tell you she knew who you were. Big deal. Move on. If you like her, it's a bump in the road."

On that parting note, he leaves.

Frosted Flakes and a present for Zucchini. I need to stop being a dick and reach out to her. Because as far as gifts go, this is about as good as it gets.

Even though she didn't tell me who she was, she knows me. This proves it.

Taking it back to the locker room, I drop it onto the bench and pull out my phone and go straight to my texts to message her. Something different for us.

JASPER

Got your gift

HER RESPONSE IS IMMEDIATE.

QUINN

I'm glad it got delivered

I didn't know catnip could come in the form of a sushi toy

Dolly loves hers

I hope Zucchini likes it too

About the other night

I'm sorry, Jasper

I didn't know how to tell you who I was and
that I had figured out who you were

I didn't mean to lie to you

I'm sorry for acting like a jerk

I wanted to tell you, I really did

But would you have believed me?

Probably not

Do you think you can forgive me?

I already have

So you're still feline a connection 😼

<<head smacking gif>>

You started it, buddy

Is that what I am to you?

I hope not...

Hopefully my good humor wasn't what
made you hesitate

It was my past

Are you done being hesitant? Because I
want to *officially* meet you and not have
you hesitate

No more hesitating

I really like you, Jasper, and I don't want to screw this up again

Dinner?

Really?

Yes. No more hesitating

How about tonight then?

I'm free

How about my place?

Considering you might cause chaos anywhere we go, it might be the safer bet

Only because I get to meet Zucchini

She'll be happy to meet you too

You still have my address from before?

Yes

No more ghosting

I'll be there

Good

Because I'd hate to rename you Casper The Friendly Ghoster

Aren't you funny

There's more where that came from

I can't wait

Chapter Eleven

JASPER

It's six fifty-two. Quinn is supposed to be here at seven.

Eight minutes.

It's still early. I shouldn't be worried that she's changing her mind, but I can't help it. I don't know if I could take her not showing up again.

I hate that I'm so nervous for this date.

I mean, are we even calling it a date? I don't know, but I don't want to do anything to make her change her mind.

Because I want Quinn.

Fuck, I don't remember the last time I've ever wanted someone so badly. Zucchini is happily perched on the back of the couch, tracking my pacing in the living room. Hockey highlights play in the background on a low hum. Not even that can distract me from Quinn coming here tonight.

Six fifty-nine.

One minute to go.

Please don't be late.

I watch the seconds tick by as it gets closer to seven. Until the shrill buzzer of my front door goes off.

Thank fuck.

"Quinn?" I press the button and ask over the intercom.

"It's me."

"Come on up."

I buzz her in and open the door. I don't care if I look eager. Considering I've wanted to meet her for months, she knows how I'm feeling.

The ding of the elevator echoes on the floor as I spot her, turning both ways before she sees me.

A smile lights up her face.

Fuck. I forgot how beautiful she is. Seeing her at the gala pales in comparison to now. Dark jeans show off her curvy hips, and an orange sweater hangs off her shoulder. As she gets closer and closer, her face isn't as made up as the night I discovered who she really is.

"Hi there."

Even her voice is better than that first night we met. Deep, sultry. No wonder she's a famous pop star.

"Hi." I drink my fill of her one last time before pushing open the door behind me wider. "Come on in."

Her perfume wafts over me as she walks in, a plastic container in her hand.

"Talk about a great view."

Her eyes flit over to the skyline out the window.

"It's why I wanted this place."

Quinn spins on the spot. "So you could watch football games without having to actually go to the game?"

"Not quite." I walk toward her and pull the container out of her hand. "I like the views of the city from up here."

"It's pretty great," she says. "But too close to the main drag for me."

"And here I thought—" Quinn's brown eyes widen before I can finish my sentence. "And I've lost you."

"She's adorable, Jasper."

She finds Zucchini on the couch, staring at her. Picking her up, Quinn rubs her face into my cat's soft fur.

"Sounds like she likes you too."

"You both have good taste then."

"Can I kiss you?" I blurt out before I can stop myself.

Way to play it cool, you idiot.

Grabbing the front of my sweater, she pulls me close. "I thought you'd never ask."

Her tongue darts out to wet her lips, and fuck… I can't believe the moment I've been dreaming about is finally here.

I want to savor it, but seeing in those eyes of hers how much she wants this? I close the distance.

I need to taste her. See how soft her lips are.

Capturing her bottom lip with my teeth, her quiet moan flows through me. Fuck. Sinking my hand into her hair, I tilt her head to a better angle, sealing my mouth over hers.

It's heaven. I've never felt anything better in my entire life. The softest lips open as I slide my tongue along the seam.

She tastes even better. The slight taste of mint pulls me in as my tongue explores her mouth. Swallowing every gasp and moan as her body melds to mine.

I break the kiss long enough to pull her closer, but my feline friend breaks the mood. Zucchini hisses, jumping out of Quinn's arms and running back to her cat tree.

"Sorry," Quinn calls out to her.

"Maybe next time we shouldn't smush her between us."

Her lips are swollen.

Fisting her hands in my shirt, Quinn pulls me close,

pressing her lips to my ear. A shudder racks my body, hardening my dick in my jeans.

"There will definitely be a next time, Jasper." She steps out of my hold. "But first, dinner."

A groan slips out. "I'm fine just making out tonight. I don't need to eat."

She throws a smile over her shoulder as she steps into the kitchen like she's been here dozens of times. "You might not need to, but I do."

"Right." Adjusting myself, I head into the kitchen and set her container on the counter and open the fridge. "Are steaks okay? I guess I probably should have asked before you came over."

"Steaks are great. They'll go perfectly with what I brought."

"Why do I have a feeling you're going to say Brussels sprouts?"

"Have you ever tried them, Jasper?" she fires at me, looking around for a pan.

"Yes. How else would I know they're soggy?"

Quinn taps on the oven, turning it on to preheat as I season the steaks.

"Mine won't be soggy. You're going to at least try them for me."

Wrapping a hand around her waist, I pull her back to my front. It's a perfect fit, feeling these curves against me.

"Do I get anything for trying them?"

"What do you want?"

"You."

"Mmm," she moans. "I think I can make that happen."

"Good." I press a kiss to her exposed shoulder. "Because I don't think I'll like them."

"Want to make a bet?" Quinn turns around, a playful look on her face.

"Fuck no." I laugh.

"What? Why not? Aren't all you athletic types competitive?"

"On the ice?" I nod. "Yes, but with you? I have a feeling I'll get my ass whooped."

"You would. Because I know I'm going to win."

"See? I'm humble enough to know I'll lose."

"Fine." She pushes me back. "Go start the steaks, I'll get these in the oven, and then I'll be out, okay?"

I smile back at her, grabbing the plate. "Okay."

She hums to herself as I head out onto the terrace. Music from the bars can be heard with the echoes of people talking as they walk up and down the streets.

It's one of the reasons I bought this place. I liked the feeling of having other people around. Made it not so lonely for me.

Lifting the cover off the grill, I fire it up and wait for it to warm. There's a chill in the air, the first hint that fall is right around the corner. The cooler Nashville nights are one of my favorite things about the city.

"Beer?" Quinn comes outside, feet now bare.

"Thanks." I take the drink from her as she settles into one of the outdoor chairs.

I like that she's making herself at home here.

"Rapid-fire getting to know you," I say.

"Don't we already know each other?" she asks. "I know you love cereal, Julie Andrews, and hate Brussels sprouts."

"What if I want to know other things?" I ask.

"Like what?"

"Like…have you always wanted to be a singer? Do you want to live in Nashville the rest of your life? Favorite player on the Knights? You know, basic things."

"Yes, no, and Noah."

"Really?" I quirk a brow at her as I slap the steaks on the grill.

"You set me up for it. I think you know the answer to that."

"Good." I close the lid and turn around to face her. "If you don't want to live in Nashville, where would you live?"

"I'd move out to the country. Get away from the city."

"You don't seem like a farm kinda girl."

She nods, sipping her drink and kicking her legs out into the empty seat across from her. "My grandparents used to live on a farm. I loved their old house. It was painted red, and during the summer, we used to collect chicken eggs and sing songs together. Those are some of my favorite memories."

Resting the tongs on the table, I drop my hands on either side of her and stare down into her eyes. "I guess that's where you got wanting to sing from."

"Did you always want to be a hockey player?" she asks, looping her fingers through my belt loops.

"It was about the only thing I was good at growing up, so I figured why not?" I confess. "I don't think I'd be good at anything else."

"I doubt that." Her breath ghosts over my mouth.

"I think it's why I've stuck around so long in the league. I don't know what else I would do."

"Stick with me, kid. I can help."

"Kid? Really?"

"It was right there." She giggles and I love the sound. "Maybe you can come on tour with me."

"Like a professional groupie?" I kiss her neck before pulling out of her hold. I miss her warmth immediately.

Quinn sips her beer. "Not quite what I had in mind, but maybe if I tour again, we could work something out."

"Things are escalating pretty quickly for a first date. Already talking about going on tour together?"

Tending to the steaks, I flip them, making sure the first side is done.

"Well, we did get to know each other pretty well before said date. I'm glad you didn't give up on me, Jasper," Quinn says. "Dating in my line of work isn't the easiest."

Casting a look over my shoulder at her, I see she's picking at the label on her beer bottle.

"I know it's not always easy for us guys, but I can't imagine what it was like for you."

"I—" Before she can finish her thought, the timer on her phone beeps. "Brussels sprouts are done. I'll go grab everything."

"Okay."

I watch her go, studying her curvy frame. God, I'm really hoping this night goes well. I've wanted Quinn for as long as we've been talking. *Craved* her.

I'm hoping that tomorrow I'll be making her breakfast before heading in for an early workout before our game.

"These smell amazing, and if you don't like them, you're going to break my heart." Quinn sweeps back out onto the terrace with a steaming bowl of something that smells pretty damn good in one hand and the plates and silverware in another.

"How'd you make them? They smell good."

"It's a honey sriracha glaze. You air fry them or roast them in the oven just right and they aren't soggy."

"We'll see…"

Checking the meat, the steaks are grilled to perfection. Grabbing the plates, I put one on each and join Quinn at the table.

She leans across the table, holding her beer bottle out. "Here's to finally having a first date."

"About damn time, Bella."

"And it's about damn time you try some sprouts." She smiles at me as she scoops a spoonful onto my plate.

"You know, it's a good thing I like you."

"Why's that, Hayes?"

"Otherwise I wouldn't be trying these." Stabbing a fork into the crispy green…things, I take a bite.

"So? How do you like them?" Quinn asks, biting into her steak.

I shake my head back and forth. "Not soggy, but still can't decide if I like them."

Quinn steals a kiss. "At least you tried them."

Dinner is a laid-back affair. The two of us talking for hours about everything. It's easy being around her. I was worried that we wouldn't have the same chemistry in real life as we did when talking online.

Turns out, I had nothing to worry about.

Before I know it, three hours have gone by before we're clearing the table and taking everything inside.

"You know, the night doesn't have to end just because dinner is over." I pull her against me. I'm quickly becoming addicted to the woman in my arms. "You want to take this into the bedroom?"

"You should know something, Jasper." She spins in my arms.

"What's that?"

She kisses the corner of my mouth and pulls back. I miss the feel of her immediately.

"I don't sleep with men on the first date."

"Wait, seriously?"

She nods, grabbing her purse and heading to the front door. "Play your cards right, Jasper, and you might get lucky on the second or third date."

This is not exactly what I wanted to hear. I've got a

growing problem, and I'm going to need to take care of it when she leaves.

"I did hear one good thing in that statement," I say, closing the distance between us.

"What's that?"

Grasping her chin, I give her a quick peck. "A second date."

"Is tomorrow too soon?" She chases my mouth as I pull back from her.

"You seem pretty eager for someone who doesn't want to stay."

"I have to keep you on your toes somehow." She gives me a lust-filled smile. "Does tomorrow work?"

"I've got a game tomorrow night."

This time, I trail kisses down her jaw, pressing a warm kiss below her ear.

"What about the night after?" She breathes against me, digging her fingers into my sides.

"Another game." Fuck. I am going to lose my shit waiting for this woman.

"Think I can come over after?" she asks. "Or will that be too late for you, old man?"

I give her a playful slap on the ass, and based on the moan that slips out, she liked it. I'm filing that little fact away for later.

"I think I can muster up some energy for you, Bella."

"Good. Because I can't wait."

Chapter Twelve

JASPER

QUINN

I'm excited for tonight

JASPER

Me too

Hockey games are my favorite

That's what you're excited for?

What else is there to be excited for 😜

Oh, I don't know

Our second date maybe?

Some other things…

Is it really a date when I'm coming over
after the game?

Oh, I was planning on wining and dining
you, Bella

Oh you were, were you?

But if you're more excited for the hockey game...

I was thinking you might come over to my place

Meet Dolly

Let me wine and dine you

I will never say no to meeting Dolly

Ouch

Turnabout is fair play

Need me to pick up supplies? Size small condoms?

Size small...really? Don't you think you're funny

Turnabout is fair play

It's a good thing I like you

Good thing

See you after the game

Will you be watching?

Yes

Then you'll be my good luck charm

I'll try

I don't think I've ever had a harder time concentrating on a hockey game than I have tonight. It's late in the third period, but my mind keeps drifting back to the conversation with Quinn.

I've never wanted a game to end faster than I have this one. Boston is a decent team this year, but we're crushing them. The crowd is electric, keeping us motivated all night.

But there's only one person motivating me, and I can't wait to see her.

"Hayes, you're up," Coach Andrews calls out, slapping me on the back.

Hopping over the boards, I fly down the ice toward the action. Noah does a good job blocking an errant shot and I scoop up the rebound.

Boston's on me, but I dodge their defenders and take aim at the goal. Pulling back, I fire the puck at the net and it clangs off the crossbar before sailing in.

"Fuck, yeah!" I pump my fist as the crowd goes wild.

We're up 4-1 now with only a few minutes left.

"Great job, man," Noah congratulates me.

"Felt really fucking good."

I skate back to center ice for the puck drop as the fans keep cheering. Games like this are fun. We're playing well and the crowd is into it. I wish we had more years like this —being on a team that plays well together. Sucking? Never a good time.

The line changes and I skate back toward the bench. Coach and the guys clap me on the helmet as I take my seat.

"Way to not fuck that up, Hayes," the fan behind me chirps.

The downside to season ticket holders…always the same people around us. I get a goal and that's how they react? I don't know what it would take to impress them at this point. Hell, they'd probably be happy if I never laced up my skates again.

Swigging my water, I ignore them and watch as the rest of the game ticks by. We're able to close it out with no more points scored.

After the customary shaking of hands, I head back to the locker room. With the game over, all of my attention swings to Quinn.

Damn, she really must be a good luck charm for me. After I've taken a quick shower and changed, Coach Andrews calls all of our attention to him.

"Great game tonight, men. I like what I saw out there. Working as team, knowing where everyone is going to be on the ice. I love it. Let's keep this momentum going. I'll see you all tomorrow for practice. I know we're leaving for a road trip soon, so after practice, take the afternoon off then we'll head out."

After he's done speaking, guys start to disperse. Thank God. I'm ready to grab dinner and head to Quinn's. I don't know if going over to her place qualifies as a date, but I'm bringing dinner, so in my book, it does.

"Anyone up for a drink tonight?" Graham asks.

"I could be convinced," Bode says. "The grandmas have Caleb, and Stevie was going to have a girls' night, so I'm on my own."

"I'm out," I say, grabbing my bag.

"You are?" Marcus questions. "What are you doing?"

"Yeah, big plans?" Noah asks, arms crossed with a knowing look on his face.

"Zucchini needs me home."

"That's it?" Noah cocks his eyebrow at me.

"What's wrong with going home to my cat?" I fire back at him.

"You seem to be in a hurry to get home to your *cat*."

The fucker. Based on the conniving look on his face, he knows exactly what he's doing. So what if I haven't told the other guys about Quinn yet?

This whole thing could blow up in my face and what then? I'd have to backtrack it? Not that I think that's going to happen, but considering tonight is going to be only our second date, I don't want to push the boundaries just yet.

"Leave him alone." Graham slaps Noah on the chest. "If he wants to go home to Zucchini, let him."

Graham gives me a sympathizing look. One that tells me Noah has filled him in. Which, to be fair, I didn't fill Noah in after I met with Quinn, so for all he knows, nothing has happened.

Being superstitious about things sucks.

"Maybe we can have a fowling night in a few weeks," Marcus says.

"I'm sorry, fowling? What the fuck is that?" I ask, pulling on my jacket.

"It's like bowling, but you use a football to knock down the pins. The girls played it at a friend's house and it's all they can talk about," Marcus says.

"It might give us a more even playing field," Bode gripes. "I'm in."

"Let me know when. I'm ready to kick your ass again." I shoot him a cheesy grin.

"Way to hit below the belt, Jasper," Bode says.

"I try." I toss a wave behind my shoulder. "Until then, see you guys later."

I'm off to see my good luck charm.

Chapter Thirteen

QUINN

The mood is set. The lights are low as I sip on a glass of whiskey. A vinyl record plays in the corner—something slow and sultry. I slipped into my sexiest lingerie, something I know will drive Jasper crazy, and covered up with an oversized cardigan. No need to give it all away the moment he walks in the door. My hair is down and I put on a light coating of makeup. Nothing over-the-top.

The game ended an hour ago. He should be here any time now.

I can't remember the last time I've been so…excited. I was tempted the other night to break my rule—not sleeping with someone on the first date. The only time I've done it was with Eric. That didn't turn out how I planned, so I made myself go home.

Leaving Jasper there when I wanted to stay? It was an exercise in self-control. My body tingles with need at how much I want him.

A soft knock comes from the front door.

Finally.

Giving my hair one last fluff, I cross the living room and pull the door open. My eyes rake over Jasper. The porch light illuminates him in his suit.

Scruff lining his jaw.

Hair pushed back from his face.

Jacket pulling at his biceps.

Thick thighs straining in his pants.

Brown eyes taking me in.

Before I can say a word, Dolly makes her presence known.

"Hey, sweetheart." Jasper picks up the cat that brushes between his legs.

"And here I thought you were coming to see me."

He kisses Dolly before setting her back on the ground.

"Make no mistake, Quinn. *You* are who I'm here to see."

"Good. Because, wow." I wave a hand in front of him at the suit he's wearing. It's hard not to drool over this man.

"Wow me? I can say the same about you."

Jasper pulls me in close, and I collide with the hard planes of muscle on his chest. Reaching up, I sink my fingers into the soft strands of hair at the nape of his neck and pull him down into a kiss.

A searing hot, toe-curling kiss as his tongue strokes along mine.

"Fuck, you taste amazing, Quinn," he whispers against my mouth.

"Nice goal tonight," I whisper back.

Jasper scoops me up into his arms with ease and holds me up against the wall.

Something no man has been able to do, and I love it.

What a fucking turn-on.

"Had to impress you, didn't I?" He drags his nose along my neck.

"If that goal hadn't impressed me, you holding me like this certainly would."

His mouth captures mine again in another heated kiss. Wetness gathers in my core. I'm hungry for this man. Desperate to be close to him in every way.

My hands roam over his back, trying to find purchase wherever I can. Jasper's mouth kisses down my neck as he pulls my sweater to the side.

"What's this?" He fingers the orange lace of my negligee.

"Maybe if you'd keep going, you'd find out."

Lust drips from my voice. I want to feel Jasper's hands on me everywhere. Ripping this material from my body and having his way with me.

He sets me on my feet before I realize he's pulling away.

"What are you doing?"

It clears the fog of lust surrounding me.

He holds up a brown paper bag I missed before. "This is a date, right?"

"Right…" I'm not quite sure where he's going with this.

"Dinner first. I want to make sure this qualifies as a date so we can get to the good stuff."

I groan, watching as he kicks off his shoes and pads to the couch and drops down.

"You realize I was going to give it to you?"

He smiles back at me as he opens the bag. "I still need to eat before I devour you."

"You're mean," I whine. Grabbing my drink from the kitchen counter, I sit across from him, needing to breathe Jasper-free air.

"You don't want to sit next to me?" he asks, unwrapping a chicken sandwich.

I slide my sweater higher up my leg, exposing the flesh of my thigh. "And have you tease me? I don't think so."

He adjust himself as he chews and swallows. "Which means you're going to tease me?"

I waggle my brows at him. "Yes."

We're in a standoff, our eyes locked on one another. Heat and tension swirl around us.

I sip my drink as Jasper finishes eating and stands. Deft fingers undo the buttons on his jacket and he tosses it onto the chair next to me. Taking the time to undo the buttons on his cuffs, he rolls his sleeves up.

"Damn you, Jasper."

Electricity buzzes through me as the muscles in his forearms ripple.

"What?" he asks, dropping back onto the couch, a leisurely smile in place.

"You know exactly what you're doing."

Why are forearms such a turn-on?

"Like you don't know what you're doing over there?" he fires back at me.

"And what's that?"

"Sipping your drink. Showing me those sexy legs of yours."

"Maybe if you'd kept going earlier, I wouldn't have to tease you."

Jasper pats his lap. "Then get that sweet ass of yours over here."

Taking another sip of my drink, I stand and shrug out of my cardigan. I don't miss the way his eyes widen or the way he licks his lips. He leans forward, resting his elbows on his knees as I stand just out of reach.

"Do you realize how fucking sexy you are?" He fingers

the soft material that flutters around the tops of my thighs. "Fuck, the things I want to do to you, Quinn."

"Tell me."

Jasper takes the glass from my hand and gulps down the rest of the amber liquor. "I want to rip this thing off of you."

He stands, pulling me into him. Based on the tented material of his pants, I'm going to be well taken care of.

Fingering the orange bow that sits on my shoulder, he drags it down my arm. Goose bumps break out in his finger's wake. He finds the ribbon in the front, holding the two sides together, and unties it.

My breasts spring free as he parts the material.

"These breasts of yours?" Calloused hands squeeze them together. "I want to fuck them."

"Yes. Please, yes."

One hand drifts over the soft skin of my stomach as the other tweaks my nipple. It slips into the lacey material of the thong I'm wearing.

"I want to taste you." One thick finger delves inside me. I grab on to him, sinking my nails into him. "It looks like you're already ready for me."

"I am."

I throw my head back, letting his finger move in and out of me. When he pushes two inside, I squeeze, letting him know just how badly I need him.

"So greedy, Quinn." He nips at the tender skin on my neck. "I don't think it'll be tonight, but I want you to sit on my face. I want to feel these thighs as I make you come."

"Yes, Jasper. Yes," I purr.

"And once I've made you come, I'm going to bury my cock inside this sweet little cunt of yours and make you scream."

"Jasper!"

Holy shit. My orgasm slams into me before I can even stop it. I came. Holy shit, I came so hard at this man's touch. His hands? His words? His fingers? All of it together was the perfect recipe as I soak his fingers.

"That's it, baby. Come like the greedy good girl you are."

"Gah."

It takes everything I have not to collapse in his arms. He holds me up as I come down from the high he brought me. Jasper sucks his fingers into his mouth. I bite down on my bottom lip as I watch him.

"Fucking delicious, Quinn."

I love the way he says my name. Like he can't get enough of it.

"I want more," I whisper, trailing my mouth up the pulsing vein in his neck. I love the feel of his scruff under my lips.

Hoisting me into his arms, he asks, "Which way to the bedroom?"

I point him in the direction as I continue my ministrations on him. I have never wanted someone so badly before in my life.

I don't know if it's the connection the two of us have, or the way Jasper makes me feel safe and cared for, but I want to give everything I have to this man. And I know, *I know*, he'll give it to me in return.

Laying me in the center of the bed, Jasper stands at the foot in all his glory. The negligee lies open as he undoes his shirt, exposing a six-pack of deliciously carved abs.

Dark hair lines his chest. I want to sink my fingers into it. Kiss every part of him. I squeeze my legs closed, trying to keep it all together. I'm ready to burst at the seams again.

Jasper chucks his shirt to the side and goes to unbuckle his belt. He lets it hang open as he grabs one of my legs.

"I like seeing what I do to you."

"I'd like it even more if you did *more* to me," I beg.

"One orgasm isn't good enough?"

I shake my head. "I don't think you'd be happy giving me just the one."

Dropping to his knees, he trails hot, wet kisses up the inside of my thigh. He dodges my pussy and goes back down the other way.

"No. I want to savor every part of you before I make you come again."

"Do it."

Looking down my body at him, I notice a cocky smile on his face. "Did you not hear what I said?"

"Ugh, what?" I throw my head back in frustration.

Jasper sweeps both my legs over his shoulders. "I want to savor you, Quinn. And that means driving you crazy before I make you come on my tongue. Because when I fuck you, I'm going to have your taste on my lips."

A deep shudder racks my body. I want everything Jasper is giving me. The soft kisses on my thighs. Nipping at my hip bone. The way his fingers push my legs to the side as he swipes a wet path up my soaked thong.

"How attached are you to this?" He fingers the material of my underwear.

"Not all that attached. Why?"

His answer comes in ripping the thin fabric from my body and sealing his mouth over my clit.

"Yes!" I shout, pushing my fingers through the soft locks of his hair. I hold on as I ride his mouth.

His tongue is masterful as it strums on my clit. My heels dig into his back, urging him. I've never felt like this before. A need pulsing through me as every cell in my body rearranges itself.

"Are you going to come for me?" Jasper asks.

I squeeze my legs tighter around him, managing only a brief mumbled yes before he lavishes my clit with everything he's got.

It's perfect. Each lick and suck sends liquid fire raging through my body. His fingers squeeze and hold me tight as I combust. Stars burst behind my eyes as I come. It feels endless as wave after wave crashes over me.

Rocking back onto his heels, Jasper wipes my wetness from his mouth.

"Fuck, I don't think I'll get over how good you taste."

I give him a dazed smile. "Imagine how good it'll feel when you're fucking me while kissing me."

"Is that what you want?" He leans over my body, tugging a hard nipple between his teeth.

"Yes. Fuck me, Jasper. Fuck. Me."

Rising from the bed, Jasper shucks off his pants, socks, and boxers and…

"Damn."

His cock is perfect. On the right side of big, it's long and thick. He gives it a hard stroke as he steps closer to the bed.

"See what you do to me, baby?" He drops one hand by my head and leans close. I can feel him press into me. "All for you."

Wrapping my hand around him, I claim his mouth in a kiss as I start working my hand up and down his dick.

I swallow his moans as I wipe the precum from the leaking head and smear it along his length. I *cannot* wait to feel him inside of me.

"Condom?" he whispers, staring down at me.

I shake my head. "All my tests are negative and I'm on the pill."

"Mine are too."

I grab his dick in my hand and line it up. "Then fuck me, Jasper."

"Flip over."

I wiggle my ass, letting his dick slide through my cheeks. He gives it a hard thwack.

"Do that again!" I shout.

Because holy shit. Jasper slapping my ass? Everything about tonight has turned me on in ways I never thought possible. But that? Turns out I don't mind getting my ass slapped by this man.

He slaps my ass before fisting his hand in my hair and pulling me flush against him, thrusting his dick inside me in one go.

"Fuck!" he yells.

"Jasper!" I gasp.

Reaching behind me, I pull him down to kiss him. I need the connection. Need something to ground me as he works his way in and out of me. Slow, measured strokes fill me. Stretch me.

It's perfect.

"You feel so fucking good." He thrusts up into me. "So greedy the way you're sucking my cock into this cunt of yours."

"I'm already close," I say.

How can I be on the brink of a third orgasm in one night? I don't know if I'm ready, but I want it.

"Then hold on."

Pushing me down into the comforter, Jasper pounds into me. His hands hold on to my hips tight as he keeps thrusting and moving inside me.

The bed swallows each gasp and moan as he fucks me senseless. My fingers tighten in the pillow as my third orgasm of the night rocks me. Jasper's moves are stilted as he keeps pumping into me. It isn't long before I feel him spill inside me.

"Oh fuck, baby. Fuck!" he bites out.

My body is limp, thoroughly sated after being fucked by this man. Jasper collapses on top of me, holding me close.

"That was…"

I rest my hands over his as he peppers my neck with soft kisses.

"Yeah, I know."

Nothing else needs to be said. Because it was perfect.

Pulling out, Jasper heads to the bathroom and comes back with a washcloth in hand. The tenderness with which he takes care of me has tears prickling my eyes.

I don't know why I waited so long to give this man a chance, but I'm thankful I did.

Kicking the comforter down around my feet, I pull the sheets back and crawl under. Jasper slides in next to me.

"Rest up, Quinn. Because I plan on doing that again."

How many earth-shattering orgasms can one woman have in a night? I'm about to find out…and I can't wait.

Chapter Fourteen

Stretching out, I hear the soft pitter-patter of feet coming from the kitchen. *Dolly*. I have no idea what time it is, but I know it's early because it is still dark out. Peering over at the sleeping form next to me, I see that Jasper is out cold. The sheet hides almost nothing as I ogle his body—soft breaths coming from him as one arm covers his eyes and the other rests on his stomach.

The same body that spent the night licking, sucking, and kissing me all night long.

Everything about last night was perfect. I could lie in bed all day staring at Jasper. I've never felt more comfortable, more at home, more safe with anyone else in my life.

Not wanting to wake him up, I grab his shirt, button it up, and pad out into the kitchen. Dolly is eating from her automatic feeder when I start the coffee. My phone is on the kitchen counter. Grabbing it, I pull up my emails. Considering the first email I get is from my attorney, I can only assume it's not good news.

The only good thing is that her email is short and to the point. Court date is set for the first week of March. A delay from when she originally thought. Prep for court to start after the holidays.

As annoyed as I am, I'm glad we have a court date. A set date that maybe all of this will *finally* go away. The law is on my side, but considering it's going to be a jury of our peers, I have no idea what is going to happen.

Will he try to charm the jury to convince them he's innocent and being framed? Will people think I'm greedy for wanting what's mine?

Every time I think about it, a sick feeling settles in my stomach.

Fuck.

The coffee pot bubbles. Grabbing two mugs, I pour myself a cup, but before I can pour the second and take it into the bedroom for Jasper, warm hands wrap around me.

"And here I thought I was going to be the one waking you up," Jasper says.

"Couldn't sleep," I say. He lifts me into his arms with ease, setting me on the counter. Sleep lines his face and pillow marks crease his cheeks. "Now I'm wishing I stayed in bed a little longer."

Jasper takes a sip of my coffee before setting it down. He kisses me and makes my toes curl.

"Waking up to you and a cup of coffee isn't a bad second." He smiles. "Although, you sounded a little grumbly when I came out."

"Well, aside from the fact that you didn't get to wake me up, I got an email from my attorney."

"Really?" Jasper takes the second mug and pours himself a cup.

I nod. "I have a court date."

"I thought you already had one?" he asks. "I know a little bit based on passing conversation from Harper and Stevie."

"Sometimes things change."

"And this is for your manager?"

I sigh, tracing a hand down his carved abs. It helps to distract me from the awkward conversation we're about to have. "Also my ex."

"Your ex."

Pushing him back, I hop off the counter. "This is a couch conversation to have." He looks confused. "I'd prefer not to have it while I'm sitting on the counter."

Taking his hand, I lead him toward the living room and take a seat. He sits down next to me, pulling my legs onto his lap.

"Okay. Tell me about this guy."

His thumbs start digging into the arches of my feet and damn, does that ever feel good.

"Eric was my manager."

"Was your manager?" he asks.

"Eric signed me when I was eighteen. It was my very first contract. He discovered me at a talent competition in Boston."

Jasper gives me a cocky grin. "I knew it."

"Yeah, yeah." I wave him off. "Ever since I was a kid, all I ever wanted was to be a singer. My parents took me to see Dolly Parton and I fell in love with her presence on the stage. The way every single person in the venue had eyes only for her. They were mesmerized by her."

"I think people can say the same about you." Jasper's eyes are soft as they look at me. "I've only seen you sing twice, but you sucked me in. I've seen how people react to your music. They love you."

His words make me blush. Fans heaping praise on me is one thing, but the man I'm intimate with? A completely different story.

"I love doing it. Seeing how people react when I'm on

stage is the most rewarding part about being in the music industry. From day one, Eric took advantage of me."

"What do you mean?"

Jasper's fingers work their way up my calves. It's like he's loosening my muscles to make it easier to tell him all of this. It's a weight I don't like carrying around.

"Before I signed my contract, everyone told me make sure you own the rights to your own music. It was something I paid attention to. When I signed the contract, that's about the only thing I did look for."

"I don't like where this is headed," he says.

I shake my head. "Everything was great for those first two years. All the money was going into producing my albums and getting my name out there. It's about that time we started dating. Musician and her manager—seems like it'd be an epic love story."

His hands stall. "And I'm guessing that's where it all went wrong."

I nod. "Eric got me into all the right places, so when that first album dropped and my single hit the top ten, I was on cloud nine. Appearances on TV shows, meeting the right people, opening for one of the biggest bands in the world? I didn't think it could get any better. But then I got my first royalty check and to say it was lackluster is an understatement."

Jasper growls, not interrupting, but I can sense his anger with Eric.

"I made pennies on what I was bringing in."

"What happened to it?"

"When I asked Eric, he said it all went to cover production, tours, marketing, blah, blah, blah. Being young, naïve, and in love with him, I believed him. But as I got bigger and headlined my own tours, the checks got smaller and smaller. I knew something was wrong."

"God damn it. If I ever see this man, I will punch him in the face."

"Believe me, I want to. He was embezzling and stealing from me. His lawyer got him out of jail, but the trial is coming up soon and it's going to be hard because my attorney is still having trouble tracking down where all the money went."

His hand tightens around my calf in a protective way. I love that feeling. Feeling safe and protected with him. Something I never felt with Eric.

"This guy is an asshole."

Crawling over and settling on his lap, I wrap my arms around his shoulders and cup his cheek. "No punching is needed, but I love that you want to defend me."

He links his hands behind my back, settling just above my butt. "I'm sorry that you have to go through all of this."

"It kind of sucks. Until all of this is resolved, I'm in limbo. No manager. No contracts. No studio to record in. I can make music here, but all the creative juices are zapped."

"Because you're so stressed," Jasper confirms.

"Yeah. It's the worst."

"Is there anything that I can do? Be your sugar daddy?" He presses a kiss to the tip of my nose. "You've already ruled out punching him, so that's off the table."

"Well, as far as sugar daddies go, you'd be a pretty good one." I smile back at him. "I just hate how young and stupid I was. Everyone told me to keep my rights, but I didn't think past that."

"Hey. You weren't stupid." Jasper's voice is firm. "He took advantage of you. Here was someone young and vulnerable, and he didn't think twice about doing what he did."

His words stir something deep inside of me. The part that made it hard to trust after Eric. It's thawing that wall around me that I've been taking down brick by brick because of this man here.

"He made it hard to trust my own judgment. I thought he was one of the good ones. I just wanted to be famous and tour the world."

Jasper smiles, pressing a kiss to my palm. "Well, at least he did that. I know you're famous and I don't really follow pop music."

"You're going to have to start. I mean, how can you be my groupie if you don't know any of my songs?"

"Hey." He points a finger at me. "I know the one you sang—"

"You better not say at the game," I joke. "Everyone knows the national anthem."

"I was going to say the one with the flowers in the cracks from the gala."

"'Wildflowers in the Weeds,' but close."

"See? I'm already halfway there."

"I can send you home with all my CDs. Play them for Zucchini so she doesn't forget who I am."

Jasper shakes his head. "It'd be impossible for anyone to forget about you."

The smile that Jasper gives me does funny things to my insides. Swirls and mushes them all up and rearranges them in a way that he completely owns. Maybe this is why I was so hesitant to meet Jasper in the first place. Because I knew once I met him, I would fall hard. Hell, texting with him over the phone, I knew I was falling. And now…now I'm so far gone for this man. I don't know which way is up and which way is down.

It's why the next confession slips out.

"You know what I always wanted as a little girl? Even more so than being a singer?"

"What?"

Jasper traces his fingers along the lines in my palm. Wrapped up with him like this, I feel safe. Like I can tell him anything and he'll never judge me.

"A red farmhouse on a big piece of land away from everyone. I wanted to raise chickens and have some horses. I wanted to run barefoot through the grass. Have a tire swing and let the wind blow through my hair."

"You want to be free."

"Yeah."

"I'm sorry, Quinn. I wish I could whisk you away from all of this."

"You being here helps more than you know."

"I only wish I could be here for you more."

I smile at him, stroking his cheek. Memorizing his handsome face. Every little detail that I never want to forget. "Life of an NHL player and all."

"You know, it's been pretty hard these last few years. Getting older and trying to keep my place in the league. I guess we're more alike than we thought."

"Both fighting for our place in our respective careers."

The corner of Jasper's mouth quirks up into a half-smile. "Well, if I had to fight for things with anyone, I'm glad it's you."

"Me too."

Happier than I could ever admit, I don't think I could even put it into words. Because having Jasper on my side through this whole ordeal will get me through it.

Come hell or high water.

Chapter Fifteen

JASPER

"I appreciate all of you coming to Chloe's store opening tonight," Dax says, holding his drink up in a toast.

Sitting around a back table at the Sin Bin, it feels like it's been ages since all of us have been here. With the guys all partnering off, we tend to go to their places now.

"Did Chloe not want you there to help?" Bode asks, sipping on his own cocktail.

Dax smacks his lips. "No. She wanted the girls there to put the finishing touches on everything. Said she wanted to surprise me."

"Hey, it's going to be great," I say. "After all you two have been through, you deserve this."

It's been a long few weeks. With lengthy road trips and Quinn prepping for trial, our time together has been limited. If we were out in public together, there is no place I'd rather be than having her by my side tonight.

But we can't.

Instead, I'm here with the guys wishing she were going to meet me later. Hell, it's not like I can even buy her anything because it'd look suspicious since I haven't told any of them about her.

Well, except Noah. Who surprisingly has kept his mouth shut so far.

"Like I said," Dax continues, "I'm glad you could all come tonight. I know it's not easy taking time away from your families."

"Hey, you're our family too," Bode says. "We love you, man."

"Aww, what a sap you've become," Noah chirps.

Bode brushes him off. "Fuck off. I'm a changed man."

"Don't listen to him." Marcus pins Noah with a look that tells him to cut it out. He ignores it.

"I guess that face only works on your kids." I laugh.

"And here I thought I had more influence over you guys." Marcus shakes his head. "That always works on my kids."

"Because you can take away screen time," Dax says. "I'd be scared if you could do that."

"Maybe I need to threaten to take away your phones then," Marcus states matter-of-factly.

"Nice try, Marcus," I say. "I don't think you're getting any of our devices."

At least not mine. Because for the longest time, it was the only way I could communicate with Quinn. Given that she can't be here tonight, it's the only way I can talk with her.

"Why would you need your phone?" Noah asks, glancing over at me. "Got a hot date or something?"

Asshole.

"Why would I need a date when I'm hanging out with you idiots tonight?" I give him a cheesy, knowing smile.

"Oh, I don't know—"

Graham slaps a hand over Noah's mouth before he can finish. "Be nice. Tonight is all about Chloe and Dax."

"Well, mostly Chloe," Dax says, a lovesick look washing over his face. "It's her big night."

After having to deal with Dax's douchebag of a brother, Duncan, and all his bullshit, these two deserve time to just be together.

Is this what it's going to be like for Quinn and me? The two of us getting through all the bullshit of her trial and ex and finally getting to be together? I have no idea how long the trial is going to take, but I'll be by her side every step of the way.

"Wings and nachos." The waitress comes by, dropping our appetizers in the middle of the table.

"Thank God. I'm starving." Graham helps himself to a nacho, overloaded with cheese, sour cream, and guacamole.

"You know Chloe is going to have food there tonight, right?" Dax asks, grabbing a chicken wing.

"Graham didn't get lunch in after practice. We didn't have much time at home." Noah pats his stomach. "Let him be."

"For someone that gives so much grief, you sure don't let anyone give it to you," I jest.

Noah turns to me, sipping on a beer. "I could give you so much more grief if I really wanted to, Jasper."

"I'm good. I don't need any more," I mumble.

The last thing I want is Noah blurting out who I'm dating. In the middle of a crowded bar on Broadway is not the place for the guys to find out I'm dating Quinn.

Or Genevieve as the world knows her.

"At least it seems like the fans aren't giving you as much crap anymore," Marcus says.

"Because you're always on the ice when they're chirping at me."

"I'd like to see them play," Bode huffs. "It's not easy trying to play on skates. Trust me, I keep trying to get Caleb out on the ice, but I don't think it's working yet."

"Why don't you wait until he has all his teeth before trying to get him in skates?" Marcus asks, laughter evident in his tone.

"Sue me. I want to carry on the Adams name and have Caleb be the second-best player ever for the Knights," he says.

"Assuming you're the first?" Noah asks, scooping nachos out onto a plate.

"Duh." He rolls his eyes at us as we all dig in to the food on the table.

Having only had time for a quick shower after practice, I came straight to the bar. I scarf down what I can, getting a warning from Dax that we need to leave soon.

Fine by me. The sooner we leave, the sooner I can get to Quinn.

By the time we leave, downtown is bustling. It always is. Even on a Thursday night, people are spilling out of bars as music competes to be heard.

Dax leads the way as he steers us off the main drag and onto a side street that is no less busy. A sign hangs over a door, painted in pink, reading "Charms by Chloe."

"This is it." Dax swings the door open and we all filter inside.

All of the guys go right to their partners. Meanwhile, I stroll around, taking everything in.

Exposed brick walls. Old Edison bulbs dropping down from the high ceilings. Hardwood floors. Display cases line both walls with tables filled with jewelry in the middle.

I let out a low whistle. "Wow, this place looks great, Chloe."

"I couldn't have done it without Dax," she says, blushing.

"You did it. You and all these amazing women helping you," he replies.

The two of them are so in love that before, it would have hurt to see. While it stings I don't have Quinn here with me, I know this is the exact type of thing she would love. That maybe once the two of us take this thing public, we can come to events like this.

Until then, I snap a picture and send it to her.

JASPER

I really wish you could be here tonight
<<picture of store>>

QUINN

I am going to have to make the trip

Send me pictures of the jewelry

You'd love all of them <<picture of rings>>

Think you could buy one for me?

Without the guys noticing?

Probably not

But hey, I'm supporting Chloe, right?

Try it and see

Are you still coming over tonight when
you're done?

Try and keep me away

"YOU REALLY MADE EVERYTHING?" I ask, fingering a ring as I stuff my phone back in my pocket.

"I did. So if there's anything you want, let me know. And I'll be taking custom orders as well, so I can always make something for you."

"You know,"—I smile at her, examining a gold ring with a large black stone set in it—"I don't have anyone I could give this to, but can I buy it to support you?"

Tears well in her eyes. "You really don't have to do that, Jasper."

"I want to."

I have no idea if it will fit Quinn or not, but we'll see.

"What are you buying?" Noah asks, dropping his elbows onto the counter as Chloe rings me up.

"Would you quit it?" I hiss.

"Quit what? I'm only asking you what you're buying." He waggles his eyebrows at me.

Chloe eyes the two of us, but passes over the bag as she takes my card and runs it through the machine.

The rest of the guys are standing around together in one corner as a few people drift inside. I head over to them, doing my best to ignore Noah and his not-so-subtle hints.

"What'd you buy?" Marcus nods at my bag.

"A ring. Wanted to support Chloe, even if I have no one to give it to."

"Maybe I can find a teacher at school to set you up with," Harper says. "A guy like you? They'd love you."

"Maybe," I say, not putting much effort or commitment into my answer.

I don't want to jinx anything. It's still early. With both of us in the public spotlight, our relationship is going to be under a microscope the minute we're seen together. Me? I'm not that big of a draw. It's all Quinn.

Right now, it's easier to let this thing grow, just the two of us. Even though the guys will be supportive, I still want to keep this to myself.

What we have is special. And I'll protect it as long as I can.

Chapter Sixteen

"You have a lot of bags for someone who can't spend the night tonight."

Jasper is loaded down as he comes in my front door, one oversized bag in his right hand and a tiny bag, stamped with a store logo, in the other.

"Hi to you too." He leans down, dropping a kiss on my lips.

"Hi." I take the large, canvas tote from him, hearing items knocking together as I set it on the counter. "What is all of this?"

"Well, this"—he hands me the small bag—"is for you. The other is what I plan on doing tonight."

Pulling out a piece of pink tissue paper, I open the jewelry bag and a gold ring drops into my palm. "Chloe made this?"

"She did." Jasper takes it from my hand and slides it down my middle finger. A perfect fit. "I got it under the guise of wanting to support her. Noah is about ready to burst and tell the guys, but he's keeping it in check."

"Are you sure?" I wiggle my fingers, letting the light catch the black gemstone.

"We'll see." Jasper scoops me up and kisses me.

Properly.

Teasing ever so slightly, I open for him. The sweet taste of mint lingers as our tongues fight for control.

"Mmm," I moan.

Every kiss with Jasper is better than the last. It might be my favorite thing about being with him. The sex is crazy good, but kissing him? There's something about a great kiss—a man who knows what he's doing—that is just as good.

And Jasper?

He knows what he's doing. The way his hands explore my body. Alternating pressure. Nibbling on my bottom lip.

I want more.

"Jasper," I purr.

"Not yet," he whispers against my swollen lips. "Later."

I groan. "What is better than kissing and sex?"

He steps back, adjusting his pants. "Considering I can't really take you out, we have to have 'real' dates."

"Okay?" I question.

Jasper grabs the bag from the counter and two beers from the fridge. He swings the bag over his shoulder and gives Dolly a scratch behind the ears as he heads out to the patio.

"C'mon."

The bag spills open as he drops it onto the grass in my fenced-in yard.

"Bowling pins and a football? What in the world?"

I take the proffered beer as he moves away from me.

"It's called fowling. Marcus was saying his girls love it, and I thought it might be something fun for us to do. You know, since we can't actually go bowling on a first date."

This man remembers everything. If I once told him my favorite ice cream flavor was pistachio, he'd remember. If I said I loved the Black Diamonds more than the Knights, he'd accept it. This is just the kind of man Jasper is.

How did I get so lucky to match with someone like him?

"How exactly do we play?" I ask, stepping onto the grass as he sets up ten pins.

"Well, normally we'd each have our own set of pins, but the point is you get two throws to knock all the pins down."

"So bowling with a football," I clarify.

"Exactly."

"I feel like you're going to win," I say, eyeing him up and down.

He looks sexy as hell in a black sweater, light jeans, and loafers. His hair is slicked back—he dressed up for the event tonight at Chloe's store. I love that he puts in an effort for his teammates and their partners.

It shows what kind of person Jasper is. That I made the right choice.

"Why's that?" he asks, walking toward me and pulling me in close.

"You're an athlete and good at these kinds of things."

"I play hockey, Quinn. Not football."

"Still doesn't mean you don't have good arm strength."

He kisses me again, swirling all my brain cells together so I can't think. "You've never complained about it before."

"Mmm, no, I haven't." I open my eyes to find a knowing grin on his face. "What were we talking about?"

"You'll get ten points to start." He steals one last kiss before slapping my ass. "You're up, Bella."

"That was definitely unfair." Jasper tosses the football to me. "Kissing me to distract me? That's low, Hayes."

"You got ten points." He sips his beer. "Now, quit stalling and let's see what you can do."

Sports was never my thing growing up. My parents always said I could sing before I could talk, and I've been doing it ever since. Sports never came naturally to me. I'd rather be in the stands watching.

Pulling my hand back, I toss the ball at the pins set up twenty feet from me. Two pins fall over while a third spins around before falling over.

"Hey, look. You got three." There's a shit-eating grin on his face.

"Yeah, yeah."

I stalk toward the pins and grab the ball, ready to take my second turn. I don't do any better, only knocking down two.

"Five is respectable."

I can hear the laughter in his voice as he sets the pins up. I smack his ass on the way back to the table to grab my beer and watch him take his turn.

"Let's see if you can get a *respectable* number."

Jasper blows me a kiss before taking his spot. He readies his stance and pitches the ball toward the pins, knocking down seven.

"Fuck, yeah!" he shouts.

"See? It's rigged."

"How is it rigged?" He jogs to get the ball and comes to stand in front of me. He tries to come in for another kiss, but I cover his mouth.

"Oh no, you don't. There will be no more distracting from you."

"Kissing you is a distraction?" he asks.

I nod. "Yes. Because it makes my brain all swirly and I can't think straight."

"Not sure how that's rigging the game, but okay."

"Because you're making it hard for me to concentrate on throwing the ball," I fire back as he takes his turn.

Of course he knocks down the rest of them.

"That's a spare."

He pumps his arm and runs behind me to grab his beer.

I huff back over to set the pins up and take my turn. A measly four pins this time.

"I think we need to play lowest score wins," I say.

"This isn't golf, Bella."

"Is it even a real game?" I jab. "Because I say we make our own rules."

"Too late for that, baby."

Jasper takes his turn again and knocks down seven. It's back and forth as Jasper cheers me on with each pin I knock down. I don't think either of us is keeping score.

I could lose one hundred times over and be fine with it because this is easy. Being with Jasper like this gives me a look into our future. Quiet nights spent together doing silly things. Nights going to his hockey games. Him watching me perform.

Hopefully.

I push that thought away. I don't want any of the upcoming trial to ruin our night together.

"Okay." Jasper rubs his hands together. "Think you can get a strike?"

I rest the football against my hip. "If you help me."

"Alright." He sets his drink down and hurries over to me. "Let me see if I can make this easier for you."

Jasper stands behind me, adjusting my hips. His one

hand stays on my hip while the other trails up and down my bare arm.

"You're going to want to pull this arm back," he continues.

"Uh-huh." It's hard to concentrate with the soft touch of his hands on me.

"And once you're ready, turn your hips and put some power into your throw before releasing."

"In my hips?" I wiggle them against him and feel his cock harden. "I think you're saying these things on purpose."

"Oh, yeah?" He brushes the hair off my neck and drops a warm kiss where my shoulder meets my neck. "And what do you think I'm trying to do?"

"I think you're trying to help but really don't want me scoring any points."

"But according to you, we're playing lowest score wins."

I feel his smile against me.

"And if we're playing by your rules, you're crushing me."

"I haven't been keeping track."

"Of course not."

"I'll give you some motivation if you want to try and get all of these pins knocked down." He slides his hand up to my stomach and pulls me back flush against his front.

"I'm listening," I whisper, sinking into his warm hold. A cool breeze sweeps through the backyard.

"If you knock down every single pin, I will take you to your room and do whatever you want me to do to you."

"Whatever I want? Hmm." I tap my finger against my chin.

"Whatever you want, Bella. Anything."

"Okay. Then get out of my way."

He steps back, taking his warmth with him. Jasper-free air lets me breathe so I can cool my racing thoughts.

A strike to go inside with Jasper?

I concentrate with all my might. Pulling my arm back, I toss the ball as hard as I can. Eight pins knock over, with the ninth spinning before tipping over into another before it falls. The last pin bobbles but stays upright.

Before I can say anything, Jasper runs over and knocks it down.

"Looks like you got a strike to me."

Chapter Seventeen

QUINN

Before I can get inside, Jasper lifts me over his shoulder and carries me through the door.

"Someone's excited." I laugh, slapping his ass.

He returns the favor, the sting vibrating through me.

"When you grind that pretty little ass of yours into my dick, I get antsy."

He doesn't stop until he's deposited me on my feet in my bedroom and closes the door behind me.

I wag my finger at him, beckoning him close. "It's not like you weren't driving me crazy all night."

"Well, you get whatever you want now, Quinn. What will it be?" Heat coats his voice.

"I have a few ideas." I tap my finger to my chin. Dropping to the bed, I cross one jean-clad leg over the other. "Lose the sweater."

Grasping the back of his neck, he pulls it up and over, tossing it on the floor. "What next?"

"I want to admire these abs of yours."

"Turning me into eye candy?" He quirks a brow at me, rubbing his dick through his jeans.

"None of that." I wave his hand away. "That's my job."

"Fuck. Yes."

Jasper balls his hands into fists at his side.

Standing up, I circle around him. I love getting to be in control like this. His dick is tenting his jeans as I get close, and his nipples harden as I drag a finger down the center of his chest.

"You are without a doubt the sexiest man on the planet." I drag my finger over his abs, near the V of his hips and around his back. "There is so much that I want to do to you that I'm having trouble deciding where to start."

"Tell me then."

I go back to standing in front of him. "Take off your pants. Only your pants."

He does what I ask in a heartbeat, kicking off his shoes and socks before taking off his jeans and adding them to the growing pile of clothes on the floor.

"What next?"

Licking my lips, I drop to my knees. "I want to tease you."

I press kisses to the soft fabric of his boxer briefs as his moans hit me. If possible, his cock gets harder.

I pull the material down and tuck it under his balls, and his dick springs free. Precum leaks from the head.

I haven't had the chance to taste him. To feel the weight of his cock in my mouth.

Licking my lips, I take him as deep as I can in one go. I choke the slightest bit as he bumps the back of my throat. My eyes water as I adjust to his length.

The growl that comes from him has my pussy growing wet. I love the power that comes from getting on my knees for this man. He is just as delicious as I knew he would be.

I suck him down, adding my hands to work him over. I

pull off and swirl my tongue on the tip before sucking him back in my mouth. As I bob up and down, his hands fist in my hair. The sting of pain edges me on.

"Fuck, I don't want to come down your throat," Jasper moans.

Rocking back onto my heels, still fully clothed, I glance up at him. "You don't?"

"No."

"Would you settle for coming on my chest?"

"What?" His voice is lust-filled, gravelly as I stand.

Unbuttoning my shirt, I toss it on the floor. "Care to fuck these?"

I squeeze my breasts together.

"Fuck, yes."

Jasper crashes his mouth against mine in the hottest kiss of my life. Sweeping me into his arms, he carries me over to the bed and rests me in the center before stripping out of his boxer briefs. My hands roam his naked body.

His muscles jump under my touch as his hands explore my body. My nipples are hard as he plucks at them through the lace fabric of my bra.

"Do that again."

"I love how responsive you are to me."

"It's because you know exactly what to do to make me feel this good."

His mouth moves down my neck, licking and sucking. His teeth tug the cup of my bra down and he lavishes my nipple with attention.

"I can't wait to fuck these breasts of yours. So fucking perfect, Quinn."

"Then do it," I egg him on.

"Not until you come at least once."

"Urgh," I groan. "Aren't you ready to come?"

His dick is poking into my leg, hard and leaking.

"I can wait. All that matters is you."

"Why are you so perfect?" I throw my arm over my eyes before Jasper moves it to the side.

Staring up into his eyes, an overwhelming sense of love washes over me. It's evident in the way he is looking at me that this man would do anything for me. No matter what.

"Because this is how you deserve to be treated, Quinn. Like the incredible woman that you are. Not only in the bedroom, but everywhere."

Grasping his cheeks, I pull him down for a kiss, soft and languid. Jasper Hayes is the most perfect man I've ever met, and I am completely, totally in love with him.

Not that I am going to tell him while we're in bed, but soon. Because someone as good as Jasper deserves to know he is loved.

Things turn heated again, my need for him growing as my pussy gets wetter and wetter.

"Jasper, please."

Pulling away from me, Jasper sits between my legs. I can't take my eyes off him and his naked form as he divests me of the rest of my clothes. His touch is reverent as he dances his fingers up my legs.

"You are the most beautiful woman in the world, Quinn. I've said it before, but damn. I'm so lucky to be with you."

"Then be with me."

Jasper leans over and closes his lips over my clit.

"Fuck!" I shout.

The strum of his tongue against the bundle of nerves has me squeezing my thighs around his head. His touch is so damn good, I can hardly stand it.

"Jasper. Jasper, Jasper, Jasper…"

I keep muttering his name as I sink my fingers into his

hair. Waves of pleasure threaten to pull me under as he thrusts his fingers inside me.

"Come on, baby. Come for me," he demands. "Fucking come for me so I can fuck those pretty little tits of yours."

My eyes lock on to his. It only takes a few more licks and twists of his fingers before I'm relenting to the euphoria inside me.

"Jasper!" I shout his name like it's the only word I ever want on my lips.

"Yes, baby," he purrs against me. "That's it."

The orgasm feels endless as I ride it out with Jasper's mouth on me. I don't know how long it lasts, but my body is spent in the best way.

"Do you know how good you look right now?" He kisses his way up my body. "Fuck, I almost came from watching you come, Quinn."

"Mmm. Then get up here and do it."

"Do you have lube?" he asks.

Nodding, I point to the nightstand. "I picked some up just in case."

Jasper leans over to grab it, popping it open and squeezing it onto his hands before rubbing it in. Goose bumps break out over my skin as he lathers the tender skin of my breasts. His thumbs roll my hard nipples as he licks his lips in anticipation.

"You ready?" Jasper gives himself a long, lazy stroke. More precum is leaking from the head of his cock.

"Yes."

I push my breasts together as he slides his dick through the opening. His cock bumps me in the chin as he rests his weight over me.

"Fuckkkk," he groans.

Holy shit. The feel of him moving between my breasts

is like nothing I've ever felt. It's making me even more wet than I was before I came.

Jasper's moves are slow and steady. Cum starts to mix with the lube as he stares down at me.

"This feels amazing, Quinn." His hands come down over mine, squeezing my breasts even closer together. "So fucking good."

"Yes. I want you to come all over me."

"I plan on it."

His moves become more hurried. Angling my chin, I try to swipe my tongue over the head of his dick to taste the cum there, but all it does is spur him on. Only a few more thrusts and Jasper is exploding. Long ropes of cum land all over my chin and chest.

"Fuck. Fuck!" he bites out, throwing his head back in delight.

I taste what I can before he collapses on the bed next to me.

Both of us are equally spent, breaths shallow.

"That was…"

"So fucking perfect, Quinn."

"Yeah."

Jasper pulls me into his side, neither one of us having the energy to move. His hands play with my hair, lulling me into a dreamy state.

"I'll get you cleaned up." He presses a kiss to the crown of my head.

"You sure you can't stay the night?" I watch, his firm ass on display, as he heads to the bathroom.

"I mean, if I do, I have to be up early to go home before practice to grab my things and take care of Zucchini."

"Hmm, okay. Maybe next time you can just bring her over and leave from here."

"Definitely."

Jasper's touch is gentle as he cleans me up with a warm washcloth before sliding into bed next to me.

"Make sure you get a good night's sleep before practice."

"Fucking best orgasm of my life? Yeah, I'll sleep well. Now, go to bed."

"Okay."

Curling up into Jasper's side, there is nowhere else in the world I would rather be than in his arms. I don't care what is going on in my life at the moment because being with him?

It makes all the noise go away.

And it makes me love him even more because of it.

Chapter Eighteen

QUINN

JASPER

See you after the game tonight 🤍

QUINN

I can't wait

It's been too long since I've seen you play

I mean, you are my good luck charm

You're the reason I've been playing so well

Well, better than normal

You're looking great out there

You have to say that

Do I?

You know I would tell you if you weren't up to snuff

Which oddly makes me feel better

No sugarcoating things

> But I also won't heckle you

Which is why I like you better than our fans

> The bar really is low

Not heckling me and wearing my jersey

I'm happy

> <<selfie here in jersey>>

Then it's a good thing I've already got this one

And now the bar has been raised

> See you at my place after?

I'll be there

Strolling down Broadway, with my hair twisted into a braided bun and a Knights cap pulled low over sunglasses, I blend into the crowd.

These are my favorite kind of days—no one spotting me and being able to come and go as I please. With the game starting in an hour or so, I wanted to hit a few shops before heading over. The less time there is before the game starts, the less time to mingle and make awkward small talk.

Because if it's not about my trial, it's about when I'll return to music. It's why I wished we could settle out of court so it wasn't blasted for the public, but that didn't happen.

People might have the best of intentions with their questions, but it stings. Because with a court date pending, and no appearances scheduled because of it, I have no answer for them.

I'm in limbo until then.

Finding the right address, I push open the door, warmth and the smell of cedar surrounding me.

"Hi there." A woman with long, blonde hair that I recognize from the gala greets me. "Welcome to Charms By Chloe."

Chatter filters through the store with its high walls and bright lights. Tables sit in the center of the store, filled with velvet trays of gleaming silver rings. Glass display cases line the walls, filled with necklaces and bracelets.

After Jasper got to attend her soft opening with the guys, I figured I'd stop by and support her. I mean, supporting a local business of a friend of the guy I'm falling in love with? Not a hardship, considering I love jewelry.

The woman behind the counter brings a small basket over to me. "If you need any help, I'm Chloe. If you need a different size, I can see what I have in back."

"Thank you so much."

Her own jewelry is stunning. Silver rings with different stones. Flower earrings. It's quirky and perfectly put together at the same time.

"All of these are beautiful," I say. "Did you make them all?"

"I did."

"Wow, that's incredible. I don't know how you do it."

I finger a silver ring with intricate flowers carved into the metal, holding a single stone in the center.

"It was a lot of trial and error, but once I got the hang of it, it was easy."

"I can only imagine."

"I won't bother you." She smiles at me. "But I'm right over there if you need anything."

"Thanks."

She goes back over to help another customer as I take in everything she has to offer. If I'm not careful, I could buy every single thing she has here.

No matter what size, shape, or color, I always have at least three rings on each hand. It's almost like they're my shield against the world. Although one catches my eye.

Trying it on, it's a bit too small. Seeing there aren't any others, I walk up to the counter.

"Do you have any other sizes in this one?"

She smiles as she takes the ring from my hand. "I sure do. I can't keep this one on the floor."

"Lots of hockey fans, I take it?"

The ring—crossed hockey sticks with a red stone in the middle—drew me in.

"I'm a big fan of the Knights."

She pulls a tray of rings from behind the counter and offers me two. I try them both on and grab the size I need.

"I like them too." I smile at her. "Who's your favorite player?"

"Dax." Her answer is immediate. Knowing who she is, I'm not surprised. "How about you?"

"I like Hayes."

"He's a good player," she says, giving my ring a last polish, even though it sparkles. "Are you going to watch the game tonight?"

"I'm headed there next. Hopefully that ring will be a good luck charm."

"If it is, I might have to start making some for the football team."

"I'll be sure to report back, but I think I only have it in

me to support our hockey team. They stress me out as it is."

And it doesn't hurt that I've got a thing for one of the players.

"They really do. I love watching him—them play," she corrects, "but when they're losing, it's hard."

"God, it really does suck."

"You got that right. Do you care to look around anymore?"

I shake my head, noting the conversation change. "That's all. I have to head out if I'm going to make it to the game on time."

"Perfect. Do you want this wrapped up, or wear it out?"

I take the ring from her and tap my card on the reader. "I'll wear it. Good luck and all, right?"

"You're all set then. Cheer loud for me."

I smile at her. "I will."

Heading out, I put my new jewelry on and snap a picture of my hand in front of the store. *A little social media promo won't hurt.*

As I'm messing with my phone, I bump into someone. "Oh, excuse—"

Ice slides down my stomach as I see who it is.

Eric. The very last person in the world I want to see.

A smarmy grin comes over his face. "Well, well, well. If it isn't Miss Rose. What are you doing down in the city?"

I cross my arms, staring up at him. "I live here."

I don't even know what to say to this man. It's been months since I've last seen him. Hell, maybe even a year. It's hard to believe that I used to look at this man and think I was going to spend the rest of my life with him.

But now all I can see is anger, bitterness, and a touch of resentment.

"What are you doing out and about? I didn't think you liked showing your face?"

"You mean you didn't like me showing my face. Thought it put too much of myself out there for my fans."

More like he didn't want me to hear the wrong thing from the wrong person about what he was actually doing.

Like embezzling money from me.

How he's walking around and not in jail is beyond me. But bail was set and I couldn't argue with my attorney about it.

"I haven't seen you perform much of anywhere lately." He ignores my comment. "You know, I could make this all go away."

"Oh?" I quirk a brow at him. "What would that entail?"

I adjust the brim of my hat, allowing myself a better look at him. Eric is the same age as Jasper, but that's where the similarities end.

Jasper is fit and wears his age with pride. So what if he has a few wrinkles or some gray hairs? It makes him sexy.

Eric? It's like he's walking around with a layer of makeup so the world can't see the *real* him.

I can't believe I was ever attracted to him.

"You can come back and work with me. Make terrific music again. It'd be great."

"Great? Just like that?" I snap my fingers to emphasize my point.

"Don't you want that?" The grin becomes even smarmier. "I know that plastic smile of yours isn't real. Not when it comes to me. We did great things together, baby."

"I'm not your baby anymore," I snap. "Do you really think I would *ever* come back and work with you when you've been stealing from me for years?"

"I'm taking what's mine, Quinn. You need to grow up

and learn how this business works." The façade drops, annoyance sliding into its place. "How do you think you got into all those clubs to perform when you were under twenty-one? You wouldn't be where you are without me and my influence."

"That makes you entitled to my money?"

"*My* money," he corrects.

"Get fucked, Eric," I spit out, brushing past him to leave.

"Now, now. Is that really the way you should talk to me?"

He stops me with a hand on my shoulder. Not hard, but certainly unwanted. It sends rage coursing through me.

"If you don't want me to make a public scene, I suggest you take your hand off of me. *Right now.*"

He steps back, hands splayed in defense. "I wasn't doing anything. But you should think about my offer."

"And if you want to talk anymore, you have my lawyer's number."

This time, I leave without him stopping me.

"Is that really how it's going to be?" he calls out after me.

I ignore him. Anger rages through me at running into him.

I hate him more than anyone else on the planet.

The man who thought I should be ashamed of my size and my curves. Who tried to mold me into his version of a pop star.

I pushed back and didn't let him steal who I was. Turns out, he found other ways to steal from me.

He was someone I never should have gotten into bed with. Both personally and professionally.

It's why it was so hard to trust Jasper at first. Eric made it hard to give my heart away. I know now that I had nothing to worry about with Jasper. He is who he says he is.

Which makes me quicken my pace to get to the game and put that entire interaction with Eric behind me.

He doesn't deserve my present or my future.

That's for Jasper.

Only Jasper.

Chapter Nineteen

I fled. As soon as Nashville put the win away, I fled the arena as fast as I could. It's not like I can go see Jasper after the game because no one knows we're dating.

After running into Eric, my mind was racing.

Me with the plastic smile?

It's just like him to put all of his issues on me. The fans were—are—the best part of this business. Without them, I wouldn't be where I am. Eric was the one that always took issue with me sharing myself. Said I had to put a barrier between myself and them.

Another way he wanted to control me.

Pulling into my garage, I shut off the car and storm into the house. Dolly is nowhere to be seen. Riffling through my desk drawer, I find a blank notebook. Because for the first time in months, my creative juices are flowing. They've been shuttered away with the looming case and everything Eric put me through. It's some kind of weird karma that running into him is what brings them out again.

Plopping down on the couch, I start to write.

. . .

The cracks start to show
The mask starts to fall
Will they see the real me?
Will they still love?
Broken down and crying
I had it all
Flying so high
Until it all came crashing down
Like stars falling from the sky
Now I'm lost in the dark...
When I hit the ground
I fall to pieces
Shatter to shards
But I pull myself up
Brush it to the side
Ready to go
I hope no one can see
It's all just a plastic smile

IS IT PERFECT? No. There will be changes, but for a first run? It's cathartic. Eric telling me that I have a plastic smile?

Fuck him.

I furiously scratch out lines and add more lyrics in

while changing things up. A beat starts to form in my head as I hum a tune.

It's all coming together in my head. But the vision starts to turn. From Eric to Jasper. From anger to one of love.

Then you came walking in
Open arms, safe and sound
A place to land
The home I never had

THE WORDS FLOWING from me now feel good. Feel *right*. I don't remember the last time I was this inspired. Eric started it, but he'll always be tied to my career. Jasper? Well, he makes writing songs about love easy.

The way he cares for me. Listens to me. Just…everything. Jasper is everything.

Tearing the page out, I set it on the coffee table and start a new song.

"Quinn?"

His voice startles me, sending papers flying everywhere. "Jesus."

"Sorry." Jasper looks sheepish. "I knocked and you didn't answer."

I press a hand to my heart, trying to calm my racing pulse. "It's okay. I was lost."

"In what?"

Jasper drops down behind the couch, resting his chin on the cushions. His hair is still damp from his postgame shower. A loose lock falls across his forehead and I tuck it away.

"Writing. Lyrics. Still changes to make but…" I sigh. "It felt good."

"Is this the first time you've written since everything happened?"

I nod. "Yeah."

He walks around the couch and drops down next to me, pulling me into his lap. "Anything I can see?"

I shake my head. "Not yet. They're still too raw."

"Can I ask what prompted this?"

Jasper traces the lines on my palms. It's hypnotic.

"I ran into Eric tonight before the game."

That stops him. "Wait, you did? What happened? Are you okay?"

He squeezes me closer. A sign of strength and solidarity from him. "I'm not going to lie. It unsettled me."

"Anything I can do to help?"

"Just being here is helping. Eric told me if I put all of this behind us, we can work together again."

"He what?" Jasper growls. "That prick honestly thinks you'd work with him after everything he's done to you?"

"Trust me, it's not going to happen."

"Good." A satisfied smile sits on his handsome face. "He'd have to go through me. I mean, you can dump me, but not for that asshole."

Cupping his cheek, I draw him in for a kiss. "I don't plan on dumping you anytime soon, Casper."

"Good, Bella. Because I'm quite fond of you."

"I'm quite fond of you too. Even if you're my elder."

"The sass." Jasper laughs, slapping my ass in a playful manner.

"You like it."

"I do. I really fucking do."

"You know, there is something that you could do to help me feel better."

"Oh, yeah?" Jasper sweeps the hair off my neck and kisses my throbbing pulse. "What might that be?"

"Karaoke."

It takes him a minute to catch up. "Wait, karaoke?"

"Yes. Singing along to some of the best songs. Some beers. All very casual."

"That's what you want to do? The world's biggest pop star?"

I shake my head. "I don't wear that crown when I'm with you. Just Jasper's girlfriend."

"You're my girlfriend now? Sliding that right in there, are you?"

My fingers play with the buttons on his shirt. "Something I'm trying out. Unless you don't want to karaoke with me. Then you're just a guy I'm chilling with."

"Again, seems unfair that I'm going to karaoke with you."

"It's not like I'm performing. I've always wanted to go but no one ever wanted to go with me. I figured if someone would go with me, it'd be—"

Jasper shuts me up with a kiss. A long, slow kiss that has my pulse fluttering.

"I never said I wouldn't go with you."

"Really?"

"Don't judge me when I suck though."

"I promise." I drop a kiss on his cheek. "I won't judge." A kiss on the other cheek. "If you do suck." A kiss on the lips. The kind of kiss that is a promise of what's to come.

"Mmm, Quinn. I know you said karaoke will make you feel better, but can I do something right now to make you feel better?"

"What might that be?" I ask, wiggling against him. His

cock hardens against the apex of my thighs. That delicious dick of his that I can't wait to feel inside me again.

"If I have to spell it out, I'm not doing it right."

Shifting off his lap, I stand and hold my hand out to him.

"Then why don't you show me all the ways you're going to make me feel better."

That's exactly what he does.

Chapter Twenty

JASPER

"I still don't think this is fair," I gripe, closing the door of our private karaoke room behind me.

"Do you want to go home?" Quinn asks, grabbing the pitcher of beer and pouring a pint for each of us. "Too chicken to take me on?"

"It's karaoke. It'd be like me taking you to play hockey." I take the glass and clink it against hers.

She takes a sip, and a foam mustache is left behind. I kiss it away, tasting her lip gloss and the beer.

"We can go play hockey if you want." A happy look is on her face. "If you want to, I will do it."

"Seeing you in a pair of skates? I kind of like that idea."

"I don't know if I'll have the best balance."

I slide a hand down her back, squeezing her ass. "You'll have me to help you."

"Hmm." She taps a red painted fingernail against her mouth. "Think you have enough pull with the team to score us some ice time?"

I nip at her earlole. "Aren't you feeling sassy tonight?"

"Well, if we need to have Dax or Noah reserve the ice for us…"

"Ouch." I feign hurt. "See if I take you home after our date tonight."

Quinn bats her eyelashes at me. "You wouldn't leave me all on my own, would you?"

"Never. But I'd drop you off at home and wouldn't come inside."

"Really?" She pushes me down onto the couch behind me and steps between my legs. "You'd deny both of us a night together? A lone night that we don't seem to get enough of because you're a big hockey star and have to travel all the time?"

"You really know how to play it, don't you?"

She drops a kiss on my cheek and heads back to the platform to perform. "Yes. Because we both know that we're spending the night together."

"Damn you." I shake my head and grab my drink. "Are you going to sing for me now?"

"I need to pick a song. Give me a minute." She shakes her head as she flips through the book.

I watch her as her eyes look over each song. The care with which she's picking it. I don't know when it happened, but I have fallen hopelessly in love with this woman. Maybe it was sometime between confessing my love of Julie Andrews or that I hate Brussels sprouts, but I finally understand why all the guys would rather spend their nights with their partners.

Hell, even when we were texting together I wanted to spend all my time with her.

She smiles at me and it does funny things to my heart. Yeah, I really do love her.

"Are you going to start?"

"I can't decide with you looking at me. Too much pressure."

"Too much pressure?" I quirk a brow at her, staring her down. "Really?"

"Don't look at me!" Quinn laughs.

"What? I want to watch you sing. Hell, I've watched you sing before."

"That's before you *knew* who I was."

"Wait." I set my drink down and lean forward. "Are you nervous?"

"Kind of. I want to impress you."

Fuck, I love this woman.

"You're the biggest pop star in the world, Quinn. You've played sold-out crowds at Madison Square Garden and Wembley."

"Are you tracking my tour dates?" she asks, cocking a hip as her chosen song starts playing in the background.

"I only know these things from Harper and Stevie. They're big fans of yours."

"They are? Not you?"

"I mean…" I hold my thumb and forefinger together, leaving a little space between them. "I'm kind of a fan."

"Kind of? That's all?"

"I don't know." I lean back in my seat and rest my ankle on my knee. "I haven't had a performance to really solidify if I'm your number one fan."

"Alright, alright."

"No more delays, Quinn. I want a private performance."

Quinn shakes her hands out in front of her, and seeming to change her mind, queues up a different song. It's a familiar upbeat tune, but I can't peg it.

Quinn's entire face lights up as she starts dancing around the tiny stage to the Whitney Houston classic.

Holy shit. It's only the two of us in this tiny room, but I don't know if these walls can contain the notes she's belting out.

Fuck. She is incredible. Goose bumps break out on my skin as I watch her perform, singing her heart out about dancing with somebody. She's mesmerizing. Sure, I saw her perform at the gala, but that was before.

Before I knew that she was Quinn.

Now?

I don't know if I'll ever get enough of watching her do what she was so clearly born to do. It makes me hate that jackass Eric even more for putting her through all this shit.

She winks at me as she keeps singing and I am a goner for this woman. As the song ends, I pop up and start cheering.

"Hell, yeah! I'm your number one fan, Quinn! Woo!"

She laughs, dropping the mic onto the stand with the music.

"I like seeing you in fan mode," she says.

I pull her into my arms and press a kiss to her forehead. "Get used to seeing it, because I'm not planning on going anywhere."

"Good."

"Maybe I'll have to make a sign that says, 'Genevieve's number one fan' on it."

She smiles up at me. "As long as I get to make one that says, 'Jasper's number one fan' too."

"We can have a sign making day. Lots of glitter. Just like we made in high school."

She laughs. "Made a lot of glitter signs in high school?"

"You didn't? We had to make them for the athletic teams to support them."

"Maybe that's what you had to do when dinosaurs roamed the earth…"

"Damn." I slap her ass and send her back to the couch. "I guess I won't be making my sign after all."

Quinn drops down onto the couch and crosses one leg over the other.

"You love me and you know it."

Her eyes go wide as she realizes what she just said. Walking over, I drop my hands on either side of her and lean down.

"In case it wasn't obvious, Quinn, I am head over heels in love with you."

She fists her hands in my shirt and pulls me closer. "I love you too. More than I ever thought possible."

I slant my mouth over hers, needing the connection with her. Finally confessing how I feel to this woman? It's better than any game-winning goal I could ever make. It's the best feeling in the world.

"Now, prepare to fall even more in love with me."

"Oh, yeah? How's that?" she asks, eyes locked on me, full of love.

"I'm about to wow you with my singing."

"I'm ready."

She looks like she couldn't wipe the smile off her face if she tried.

Finding the song, I queue it up and listen as the first few notes filter into the tiny room.

I begin singing the first line to "The Sound of Music."

"Oh my God!" Quinn shrieks, kicking her feet.

I drop my voice two octaves, then sing the next line. Or what I assume is two octaves. I don't know because I'm the worst singer in the history of time.

"Yes! Best singer ever!" Quinn cheers as I continue the song. Horribly, I might add.

By the time I finish, Quinn stands and leaps into my arms.

"I am definitely your number one fan." She peppers my face with kisses. "Best rendition of 'The Sound of Music' ever."

"Obviously," I joke. "No one can beat that."

"They wouldn't even want to try."

"God, I love you," I say.

"Not as much as I love you."

I smile at her, not setting her down. I love holding her to me like this. "Are we going to be those annoying people who say I love you all the time and annoy other people with it?"

"That would require us to be in public, but when we do, we will absolutely be those people and I'm okay with it."

"Good." I kiss her again, because I can. "Now, time for you to show me up with another song."

She slides down me, and I hate the loss of her warmth. "I don't know if I can live up to your performance, but I'll try."

"Don't worry. I'll get you back once we're on the ice together."

She winks at me. "I have no doubt you will."

Damn. I cannot wait to get this woman into a pair of skates.

Chapter Twenty-One

JASPER

The horn sounds with another Dallas goal. Fuck me. The home crowd goes nuts.

It's now 3-0 in the middle of the third period. Dallas isn't the best team by any means, but tonight we're making them look like the Stanley Cup champions.

I don't know what it is, but we can't seem to get our shit together. We're not playing our best and the goals we've let in prove that.

"Fuck." I slam my stick against the boards.

"All right. Heads in the game. We're still in this. Let's get back out there and get some points on the board."

Coach Andrews is nothing but positive behind the bench. Clapping me and Noah on the shoulder, he sends us out onto the ice for our shift.

Dallas swarms us immediately as we try to take back control of the game. We don't have much to show for it as we move around the ice trying to put the puck in the net. One of our wingers gets a shot, but to no avail.

"Damn it," I mutter, trying to chase down their center

to prevent another scoring opportunity. They take a long shot on goal, but thankfully, it goes right into the glove of our goalie.

Thank God. Four goals would be near impossible to come back from. Hitting the bench, I swig some water as Marcus and Bode head out onto the ice. Marcus is able to get us on the board and give us a little momentum.

When it's my shift again, I hop over the boards and call for the puck. It gets sent over, right into the cradle of my stick. I don't need any fancy moves as I move down the ice.

I've got good luck watching me from home.

Our center is waiting at the top of the crease, and before I can get the puck off, one of their defensemen comes out of nowhere, checking me into the boards.

A nasty crunch sounds from my shoulder.

"Fuck!"

I collapse onto the ice, grabbing my shoulder to try and stave off the pain. A wave of nausea rolls through me.

"Fuck, fuck, fuck."

The whistle blows and the guys swarm around me.

"Are you okay?" Noah asks.

"Fuck, no," I bite out.

"Is it your shoulder?"

I nod. "It fucking hurts."

"Can you stand up?" Noah asks.

"Give me a second."

I breathe through the pain as I gingerly stand up. I blow out a breath, wincing as my whole arm twinges.

"Need help getting over to the bench?"

I shake my head at Noah. "Thanks, man. I got it."

Moving slower than I normally would, I head toward one of the trainers who is waiting for me and immediately takes me back to the locker room.

Never a good sign.

"Where's it hurt?" he asks as we head into the visitors' locker room.

"Shoulder."

"Okay, let's get you out of these pads and we'll get an X-ray to see what's going on."

"Okay."

I try not to let the pain show as he helps me out of my jersey and pads, but fuck, it hurts. There's already bruising and swelling. Not good.

I lie on the table as he starts the process. Noise reverberates through the locker room.

Fuck. No doubt Dallas got another goal.

It is not our night tonight.

"Alright. Give me a few minutes to review these and then I'll be back with some ice for you, okay?"

"Sounds good."

Great. Just what I need. An injury to deal with. Maybe it won't be as bad as I think. Just a gnarly bruise that will go away with some ice and ibuprofen. Something I can play through.

But the swelling tells me otherwise. I've been in the game long enough to know when things are serious.

Considering I haven't been playing my best this season and now an injury? Fuck. This stings.

"Good news and bad news, Jasper." The trainer comes back in. "You have a separated shoulder, but it isn't severe."

"Thank fuck," I breathe out. "How long will I be out?"

"Conservative side? I'd say four weeks. At least until the All-Star break."

Considering I'm not playing in it, that helps.

"What's the game plan?" I ask, taking the sling from him as he helps me into it.

"Rotate between ice and heat. Ibuprofen to help with the pain and we'll get you in for some PT to make sure you get back on the ice as soon as it heals."

"I don't want to be out any longer than I have to be."

I can hear the heckles of the fans now.

Jasper Hayes can't play hockey to save his life.

Getting injured? He doesn't deserve to be on the team.

This is why I told Quinn I hated hockey in those early conversations. No matter what I do, it's hard to drown out the voices of the people that are supposed to be your fans. I've given everything I have to this game since I was drafted by the Knights and it means nothing.

I've put my body on the line year in and year out, and now, it's finally catching up with me.

"Think you can make it back to your locker and change?"

I nod. "Yeah. I'll be okay."

I take the ibuprofen he gives me and swallow it down without water. The bright side is that we're heading home tonight.

Heading back to my stall, I find the guys already in there. Heads hang, telling me we lost the game.

Fuck.

We're still looking good to clinch a playoff spot, but it's January. It's still early.

"How are you feeling, Jasper?" Coach Andrews asks.

"I've been better." I grimace. "Separated shoulder."

"Really?" Bode asks from his spot in the locker. "Fuck, man. I'm sorry."

"How long will you be out?" Dax asks.

"A few weeks. Could be worse, so there's that."

"Damn. This sucks," Noah grumbles. "I'm sorry, man."

"Look." Coach Andrews calls everyone's attention to

him. "Tonight was not our night. I don't want us to get too down about this. We still have a great group of men and that will carry us through these next few weeks before the All-Star break. Let's rest up tonight, and tomorrow we'll study film to see what we can improve on for the next game."

Guys hit the showers as I drop into my seat, not having the energy to get cleaned up at the moment.

Hell, I don't even have the energy to grab my phone and see if Quinn texted me. Knowing her, there is a slew of messages.

"You need any help?" Dax asks.

"I'll be okay." I shake my head. "Just need a minute."

"You sure?"

"I'm sure. Fucking sucks we lost."

Dax winces. "Definitely not our best game of the year."

"Hey." Bode claps him on the shoulder. "We'll get it back. We always do."

We've been having one of the best seasons in the history of the Knights franchise. With only a dozen or so losses, our playoff standing is looking good.

Knock on wood.

"Damn right we will," I say.

With my left arm being in a sling, I start to change as carefully as possible. It's not easy with one arm, but it could be worse.

By the time I'm changed, I'm exhausted and ready to hit the bus. Dax grabs my bag for me and I follow him, finally taking out my phone.

I smile as I see the string of texts from Quinn.

QUINN

This game

Ouch

What is with Dallas tonight?

It's like they're playing for the Cup

Calm down, Dallas

It's January

Fuck, another goal

This sucks

MY SMILE GROWS WIDER at the play-by-play I'm getting of the game. I know the minute I left the game based on how fast the texts came in.

QUINN

OH MY GOD

Are you okay?

That hit was bad

They should have thrown him out of the game

Two minutes in the sin bin?

Please

I'll come down there and kick his ass

See how he likes it

THAT HAS a snort coming out of me. God, I love this woman and how readily she'll come to my defense.

QUINN

Is it your shoulder?

Your arm?

What's wrong?

Why aren't you texting me back?

Was it something worse?

Do you have a concussion and they aren't saying?

Please text me back, Jasper

I'm worried

Okay, they said separated shoulder

I hope that's all it was

The game ended fifteen minutes ago

You get another twenty before I use my pull to contact the team and find out how you are

Ten minutes, Jasper

Tick, tock

LOOKING AT MY PHONE, that was fifteen minutes ago. Stepping onto the bus to head to the airport, I walk straight to the back and take an empty seat and dial her number. She answers immediately.

"Thank God. Are you okay?"

"Sore and in a bit of pain, but I'll live."

"I was about ready to send out a search party for you."

"No search party needed." I smile even though she can't see me. "Just needed to change and get to the bus so I wouldn't be left behind."

"No concussion or anything? They said separated shoulder, but I don't know if they're lying or not."

"They weren't lying. I'll be out a few weeks, but hopefully I'll be ready to go after the break."

"Okay, good. Is there anything I can do to help?"

"Not right now. Maybe I can come over tomorrow?"

"Yes. I'll take care of you. Make sure you don't overdo it. Do you want me to go get Zucchini so you don't have to worry about her?"

"No. Maybe she'll help me feel better tonight. I'd come over to you, but that's too far for me."

"I can come to you," she says.

"It's late. You get some sleep and I'll pick up breakfast on the way over."

She laughs. "Let me guess—you're going to bring over Frosted Flakes."

"Have you actually tried them before?"

"Ugh. Not in years, but you're going to make me, aren't you?"

I smile. "Only if you want to. I was going to bring a good breakfast, but now I'm definitely making you try them."

"Fine. Only because you're injured."

"Hmm. I wonder what else I could get away with."

"That's how it's going to be?" Quinn asks.

"I might make you stay in and watch movies with me all day."

"You say that like it'd be a hardship."

"Maybe a Julie Andrews marathon."

"Again, I'm not hearing anything that doesn't sound fun. Curling up with you on the couch and watching movies? I'd take that any day of the week."

"Good. Then plan on it," I say. "I'll bring breakfast, Zucchini, and me."

"What else do I need?"

Chapter Twenty-Two

QUINN

"Are you sure you're comfortable?" I mess with the pillow under Jasper's arm. "I can get you another one."

"Stop it. I'm fine."

He looks up at me with an appreciative look.

"I just don't want anything to bother your shoulder to aggravate it even more."

"If it hurts, I'll tell you," he says. "Ibuprofen is helping. I iced it this morning and I'll throw the heating pad on it later."

"Okay."

"The only thing that will help is if you sit down and watch some movies."

"Can I sit next to you?"

He nods. "Zucchini basically slept on my head all night. It's like she knew I needed some comfort, so that'll be much better."

"I mean, I could do that too." Quinn smiles.

"I don't think that would help my shoulder because I'd be too worked up if you're sitting on my face."

She points a finger at me. "Don't get any ideas, Jasper. There will be no sex until you're fully healed."

He groans. "You're a terrible nurse."

"And by terrible, you mean the best. I'm going to make sure that you're well taken care of."

I grab the remote and turn on the first movie. *Mary Poppins.*

"Wow. We're starting old school."

I pull a blanket over the two of us as Zucchini and Dolly settle next to us on the couch.

With a cold spell working its way through Nashville and threatening snow, low, gray clouds darken the inside of my house. Dimming the lights, with remnants of breakfast scattered on the coffee table, it's the kind of morning I could get used to.

Snuggling on the couch with Jasper and our cats? Can't get much better than this. He wraps his good arm around me and tugs me close.

"You know, as much as I hate that I'm injured, it's kind of nice."

I rest my chin on his chest, looking up at him. "How's that?"

"Coach told me to rest up these next few weeks and that the trainers will let me know when to be back for follow-ups. It's kind of a nice break."

"You've been playing hard this season."

"It seems like no matter what I do after each game to recover, my body is more and more sore."

I rest my hand on his chest, rubbing it in circles. "I'm sure playing for so long has taken its toll."

"I'm thankful I've gone without any serious injuries."

"You don't consider this serious?" I ask.

"Nah. A few weeks? Nothing major. But it does make me wonder."

"What?"

"How much longer I want to keep putting my body through this."

Pausing the movie, I sit up. "Wait, are you thinking about retiring?"

"Right now? This is the first time I've even entertained the thought."

"Wow."

He rubs my back. "I'm in my last year of my current contract with Nashville, and I don't know if I have it in me to go play with another team."

"Would they re-sign you?"

He shakes his head. "Unknown. Considering my age and how I've been playing this season, I don't know."

"I don't think I can remember the Knights without you."

"Nothing's been decided. Maybe they re-sign me to a short contract and I keep playing."

"Do you want to?" I ask. "I mean, you said it yourself, it's taking a toll on your body."

"Maybe I have a future in singing." He laughs, changing the subject.

I take it for what it is and restart the movie. "Well, if I can move on from this whole mess with Eric, I'll hire you as one of my backup singers."

"Liar."

"Well, maybe a groupie. You'd make a pretty cute groupie."

"I'll bring Zucchini and Dolly with me. Get them little earphones to protect their hearing."

"That would be so fucking cute, Jasper."

"Once my arm gets better, I'll have a cat on each arm to cheer you on."

"Well,"—I laugh—"until then, I'll just give you sugar to help your medicine go down."

He tries to tickle my side as the song comes on. "Aren't you funny?"

"I mean, I don't know what kind of patient you are. You are one stubborn man, so really, I can only assume."

"I've been a good patient so far," he says.

"I have a feeling you're only being good today because I'm here. At home, you'll probably overdo it."

"I promise I won't."

I cock an eyebrow at him. "I might have to install a spy camera on Zucchini's collar to make sure."

That earns me a boisterous laugh. "Only you, Quinn. Only you would threaten me to take it easy by installing a camera on Zucchini's collar."

"It's either that or hire Mary Poppins to follow you around and make sure you take it easy."

"There is only one person I want following me around."

"Let me guess…Noah?"

"Har, har. Aren't you funny?"

I shrug a shoulder. "I try. He would make a good nurse for you. Yell at you to make sure you don't hurt yourself even more."

"He would be the worst. I wouldn't move from the couch just to make sure he doesn't bother me. Make him so bored, he'd leave."

"I take it back. Not hiring Noah then."

"Zucchini it is then." He pulls me back into his side and presses a kiss into my hair.

The cat in question comes over and sits in his lap. I scratch her soft fur as the characters on screen start singing about flying kites.

"You know, if we could karaoke again, I'd probably sing this one," I say.

"I'd love to hear it," Jasper says. "Maybe you could sing it when you go out on tour."

"I don't know if my fans want to hear me sing about kites…" I trail off.

"Babe, they love you. You could sing your grocery list and they'd be happy."

I burst out laughing. "Can't say I'm going to take that advice."

"Hey, I'm your number one fan. Would I steer you wrong?" He looks affronted.

"In this case? Yes. I think I'll stick to my songs."

"Speaking of your songs." He tucks a stray strand of hair behind my ear. "Will I ever get to hear you sing them in person?"

"You have. Multiple times."

He rolls his eyes at me. "That was before I knew you as Quinn. You were Genevieve then. Not the woman I was in love with."

"Ouch."

"You know what I mean. I was pretty much in love with you then, but I didn't know Genevieve was Quinn."

"Fair," I surmise.

"Karaoke doesn't count because they weren't your songs. I want to hear you sing for me."

"Well, maybe not today, but I can make that happen."

Butterflies swarm in my belly. The thought of performing for him makes me nervous. It's telling that I was never once nervous to perform in front of Eric. I was more infatuated with him than anything.

Jasper? I know what I have with Jasper is true love. Because there is no one else that I would rather sit on the couch and have a lazy morning with than him. Talking about retiring after twenty years can't be easy. I love that he trusts me to tell me about his future plans.

"Maybe once you're back in the studio, I can have a private show."

"If that happens anytime soon."

"It will. I have faith that everything will get resolved and you'll be singing in no time."

"I'm getting more nervous now that it's coming up," I confess.

"I'd be more surprised if you weren't nervous. But I plan on being there."

"You do?"

He nods. "Consider it our hard launch. I—"

"Wait." I cover his mouth with my hand. "How do you know what a hard launch is?"

"I'm not that old. I know some things."

I smile at him before giving him a gentle kiss, not wanting to bother his shoulder. "I'll take it. I don't know if I could get through the trial without you being there."

"We'll do it together. And once you win, you'll get back in that studio and record that song you were writing and it's going to launch you back into the stratosphere."

"I like the way you think."

"Yup." He pecks my lips before I curl into his side. "Then it'll be a world tour and I'll be right there with you."

"This is all sounding really good to me, but should we knock on wood?"

"You're starting to sound like a hockey player."

"I think it's only safe considering I still have to make it through the trial."

"We'll do it together."

"Thank you."

I don't know if I would be able to get through this

alone. Sure, I've been doing it mostly on my own since it all started, but having someone you love by your side? It makes the hard things easier.

I'll be with Jasper every step of the way as he heals from his injury. Just like he'll be by my side during the trial.

I wouldn't want it any other way.

Chapter Twenty-Three

"Pizza's ordered," Jasper calls out. "I hope you like pineapple."

Setting down two food bowls for the cats, I grab beers for the humans and head back into the living room of Jasper's condo.

"For once, we agree on something."

I hand him his drink, take my seat, and clink my bottle against his. Thankfully, he's making great progress on his shoulder and has been without the sling for two weeks now. He should be back on the ice in the next week or two.

Thank God.

"For once?" He quirks a brow at me. "Pretty sure we agree on a lot of things."

"Food wise? Hardly ever," I state.

"Fair."

"I'm glad you're up for watching the game tonight and having me over."

He smiles at me. "We'll call it hockey and chill."

I burst out laughing as I kick my legs onto his lap. "I'm

surprised you know what that means. I thought I'd have to get you a dictionary, old man."

Jasper wraps his hand around the back of my neck and pulls me in for a kiss.

"It's a good thing I love you."

"It's a good thing." I vibrate against him as he pulls back, licking my lips. "Are you sad you're not there?"

"At the game? Nah. I wouldn't have been selected anyway. Even as a backup."

Lights are flickering beyond the windows as the beginning of the game starts. Dolly walks over and curls up on the back of the couch. Zucchini takes her perch on the cat tree in front of the windows.

We've settled into a happy routine these last few weeks. With his time at the arena limited to practice times for physical therapy, we've been spending more and more of our time at his place.

While he's been gone, songs have been flowing out of me. Some angry because of the upcoming trial, but most of them are sappy love songs.

They'll need some work, but whenever I can start on this next album, it's going to be an emotional record.

Closing one chapter and opening another.

"That means you're happy watching it here?" I ask as I pull my thoughts back to our conversation.

"You mean in the comfort of my own home with my cat and my girlfriend?"

"Oh, is that what I am to you now?"

"You can be whatever you want to be, as long as you're mine."

My smile takes over my entire face. It's so big, I can't hide it. "Well, if it makes you feel better, *boyfriend*, you'd be on my all-star team."

He aims that cockeyed grin at me. The one that sends

my insides swirling and my heart pitter-pattering. It doesn't even take him smiling at me to make me feel like that. Anytime I'm with him, I feel like this.

"Again, I think you're biased, Quinn."

"Damn right I am. You're the best player in the league as far as I'm concerned."

"Think I can get you to say that on TV? Might shut some of the fans up around me."

I roll my eyes. "I'd like to see them play hockey. I mean, you're on their team. Why do they feel the need to give you so much grief?"

"It's what they do."

"Think I could get away with punching them? See if they like it. I'll take them on out on the ice. Just *try me*."

"You don't need to get into fights on my behalf, Quinn."

"Some of them deserve it. They're lucky I know how to keep my shit in check."

He waves a finger at me. "Is this you keeping your shit in check?"

"Don't mess with my man." I raise a brow at him. "I will fight anyone."

"You know." He pulls me onto his lap the best he can with one arm. "You getting all possessive like this is sexy."

The horn sounds from the TV, but I ignore it as I capture Jasper's mouth in an easy kiss. His hands rest above my ass as we start making out.

The scruff along his jaw is thicker than usual. I want to feel it between my legs. I run my fingers through the soft strands of his hair as I deepen the kiss.

This is what I love about kissing Jasper. He doesn't care if I'm in control. Each brush of his tongue against mine has my toes curling and my fingers sinking farther into his hair. His own hands leave bruising marks on my sides.

Why is kissing the best thing in the world?

"Think we've got time for a quickie before dinner gets here?"

The doorbell buzzes, ending that thought entirely. Just when things were getting good. I hop off his lap and head over to buzz in the pizza delivery person.

"That is bad timing." Jasper adjusts himself as he heads into the kitchen.

"Grab the plates. If you're good and eat your dinner, we can pick up where we left off."

"Yes, ma'am."

A knock comes from the front door and I open it.

But instead of the pizza guy, it's Jasper's teammates.

Noah, Graham, and Dax.

So much for keeping this under wraps.

Chapter Twenty-Four

JASPER

"Hey, Jasper?" Quinn's voice calls out.

Grabbing the plates and napkins, I walk back into the living room. Instead of seeing Quinn setting up the pizza boxes on the coffee table, Dax is at the door, holding five pizza boxes and standing beside Noah and Graham.

Fuck.

Fuck, fuck, fuck.

Noah has a shit-eating grin on his face, Graham looks gobsmacked, but not entirely surprised, but Dax? He looks clueless. Likely because he's been so loved up with Chloe lately.

"I'm sorry, do you know who you are?" Dax asks.

Noah smacks him on the back of his head. "Where are your manners?"

"Why aren't you freaking out about this?" Dax swings his look of shock to Noah. "That's Genevieve."

"Actually, it's Quinn to my friends," she says.

"Is he your friend?" Dax questions.

"Why don't you get your asses inside and I'll fill you

in." I sidle up behind Quinn and wave them in.

This is not a conversation to be having in the hallway in my building. I've got good neighbors, but I don't need to be airing my private life for all of them to hear.

"Do you want me to leave?" Quinn asks, dropping her voice.

I stare down at her. Her gaze is flitting back and forth between me and the guys.

"I think it'll be easier if you're here for this."

"We've been pestering him for months about if he's been dating someone. You're staying," Graham says.

I guess we're not as quiet as we thought.

"Can we at least eat while we talk about this?" I ask. My stomach gives a loud rumble. "Otherwise, I'm liable to eat one of you three and I won't be sorry."

"Works for me. I'm starving." Noah shrugs a shoulder and takes the pizza boxes from Dax and sets them on the counter. "We brought pizza over because we figured you'd be at home by yourself and want some company."

"That's nice of you," I say.

"Why are you not freaking out about this?" Dax interrupts, grabbing a beer from the six-pack Graham sets down next to the pizza. "Jasper is…dating the world's biggest pop star?"

"You say it like that's a question," I fire back at him, grabbing a slice and tearing off the end.

"I don't actually know what this is." Dax waves a finger between the two of us. "And back to why am I the only one freaking out about this?"

Noah and Graham exchange a look.

"I might have already known about it," Noah says.

"And I know because he knows," Graham confirms. "Boyfriend privileges and all that."

"Technically, I told you about Quinn. I never actually got around to telling you we were dating."

Noah shrugs before taking his plate into the living room. "The fact that you asked me for advice when you normally would have ignored me? I knew you were going to start dating."

"Wait, you knew?" Dax asks Noah. "Why didn't you tell me?"

He shrugs, kicking his feet up on my coffee table. Zucchini takes it as an invitation to curl up next to him.

"Honestly? I told Graham and then Jasper got injured and I kind of forgot."

"You kind of forgot." Dax rolls his eyes, indignation washing over his face. "I can't believe you."

"You know, if Bode were here, he'd murder you," Graham says.

"Would you really let that happen?" Noah asks.

Graham shrugs. "Depends on the day."

"Wow. Love you too, babe."

Graham blows a kiss his way as Quinn burrows into my side. "I kind of like them."

"Only kind of," I agree. "I wish I could say they're not always like this, but I'd be lying."

"It's only because they love you."

Noah perks up from the couch, where Zucchini is curling into his side, wanting all the attention. "When you tell the other guys, can I be there?"

"I should just text them and get it over with," I say, pulling out my phone.

"You are not going to text them." Quinn grabs my device from my hand. "You can tell them in person."

"Why do you have to be the adult in the relationship?"

"Because you're not?" Graham jokes.

"Careful." I flip him the bird. "I'll still kick you out."

"How did you two meet?" Dax asks. "Because it seems like these two are in the know and I know nothing."

"We met on a dating app," Quinn says.

"Which one?" Dax asks.

"Does it matter?" Graham fires back. "They met online. End of story."

Dax shakes his head. "You really need to learn how stories are told. We need details. I mean, he's dating *Genevieve*."

"You can call me Quinn," she says. "Jasper won me over with a cat joke."

"Jasper knows jokes?" Noah laughs. "Damn, I'm impressed."

"You're such a dick." I flip him off this time.

"That'd be the only way this guy could find someone," Noah snickers.

Graham smacks him on the back of the head. "I'm sorry, Quinn. I can't take him anywhere."

"It's okay. I think the two of us will be friends." Quinn takes the empty seat next to him on the couch.

"Yes!" Noah pumps his fist. "I've won over Twatopotamus here and Quinn. Maybe one day Jasper will like me."

"Don't hold your breath," I mutter.

"He secretly loves you," Quinn whispers.

"I know he does," Noah agrees.

"Okay, I don't want you two ganging up on me." I cast a wary look between them.

"But we'd have so much fun!" Quinn says.

"Yeah." Noah looks equally delighted. "I like her. She gives you shit and likes me."

"Great." I roll my eyes. "I guess it was fun while it lasted."

I take the seat next to Quinn and she moves onto my

lap. "Aww. I know you secretly love that we're all going to become friends."

I couldn't stay mad at Quinn if I tried. Not that I was actually mad. I kiss the tip of her nose. "I'm glad they like you."

"I like them too."

"I guess that means it's time you meet the rest of the guys. Maybe we'll have them over one night for dinner."

"Brussels sprouts must be had. I have to impress them."

I groan, dropping my head into her shoulder. "If you insist."

"It's like we're not even here," Noah says, interrupting us.

"Wait." Dax looks between the two of us. "Did you know it was Chloe's store when you posted about it?"

"I really wanted to go with Jasper because I love jewelry." She nods, holding up her hands to show the rings she never goes without now. "But since no one knew about us at the time, I stayed home."

"Wow." A look of gratitude comes over his face. "I can't tell you what you posting about it meant to Chloe. She loves you, and her business has exploded since then."

A shy look washes over Quinn's face. "Well, she deserves it. I love her stuff."

Dax gives me an annoyed look. "Am I allowed to tell her, or do I have to wait?"

"If I say you have to wait, will you listen to me?"

"Yes," Noah answers for him. "Because Dax doesn't want to get on anyone's bad side."

"You're on my bad side," Dax tells him.

"Why? It wasn't my news to tell," Noah says. "Be mad at Jasper."

The horn sounds again from the TV and we all look, seeing Bode celebrating a goal.

"At least we can tell them we watched the game," I say.

"They might be more upset they aren't here," Noah says. "This is a pretty good night."

Even if I wasn't planning on telling the guys about Quinn and me, I don't think it could have gone better. Dax is still in shock, but honestly? The fact that they're being their normal selves around her? I love it. They aren't starstruck. That means more than I could ever say.

It's more joking around as we eat dinner and watch the game. I remember my first All-Star game. I had the best time getting to play with some of the greatest stars in the game. But as the years went on, it was harder on my body to keep playing.

Now? I couldn't imagine spending the night any other way. With my teammates and Quinn as we support our brothers in the game.

It's perfect.

"Chloe's getting off soon. I'm going to head over there and go home with her," Dax says, taking his plate and empty beer bottle into the kitchen.

"I'd say thanks for stopping by, but this was not how I planned tonight going," I say.

"Well, I'm glad we finally know what's going on in your life," Dax replies. "You deserve to be happy."

I give him a grateful smile before pulling him in for a hug. "Thanks, man. We both do."

He says his goodbyes before heading out.

"I think that might be our cue to leave too," Graham says.

"You don't want to stay and watch the end of the game?" Noah asks.

Graham shakes his head. "Let's leave these two love-birds be. They've had a big night."

"Think I can take Twatopotamus with me?" He gives my cat a kiss on the head.

"Take her and I will hurt you," I deadpan.

"Get your own cat." Quinn laughs.

"Ugh. Fine."

"We'll have to do this again some time." Quinn gives Noah a hug before he leaves.

Noah looks over the top of her head, smiling. "She's a keeper, Jasper. Don't fuck this up."

"I don't plan on it."

"Good."

With that, the guys head out and leave me and Quinn alone.

"So that happened." Quinn laughs. "I love them."

I smile at her. "I knew they would love you."

"I am lovable." She smiles up at me.

"The most lovable person there is."

"Does that mean you're going to let me meet the rest of them?" she asks.

"I guess. Maybe after I teach you to skate, we can grab dinner and come back here and have them over."

"I'd like that."

"Good. Now, can we pick up where we left off earlier?"

Quinn wraps her arms around me, a playful look on her face. "Where exactly did we leave off earlier?"

"Let me remind you."

Chapter Twenty-Five

JASPER

Kicking the bedroom door shut behind me, I press Quinn up against it, rocking my already hard cock into her warm center.

"I don't think this is quite where we left off," she whispers against my lips.

Her pupils are wide with lust as she trails her fingers over my scruffy jaw.

"It would have been if we weren't so rudely interrupted."

"Interruptions suck." She trails her thumb over my bottom lip and I suck it into my mouth.

I swirl my tongue around the tip, watching her reaction.

"I'm yours, Jasper," she says. "Play with me. Do whatever you want with me tonight. Make me feel good."

"Baby." I capture her lips with mine. "I will make you feel fucking amazing."

Walking back to the bed, I take her with me as I sit on the edge, with her standing in front of me.

"What do you want me to do?" she asks.

"Get naked." She reaches for the bottom of her sweater and I stop her. "Slowly. Make it good."

Quinn waggles her brows at me as she pulls the sweater over her head and tosses it on the floor. She drags a finger over the cup of her bra as she spins, giving her ass a shimmy.

"You like?" she asks, unhooking her bra and letting the straps slide down her arms.

"Fuck." I squeeze my dick through my jeans. I don't want to come too soon, but damn, if this woman doesn't already have me on edge.

She turns to face me, her nipples diamond hard as she plays with them before resting her hands on my legs and facing me.

"Like what you see?"

Grasping the back of her head, I crush my mouth to hers. The kiss is hot and messy. Needy. Teeth, tongue…I don't care, I need her.

"Get. Naked."

She pulls back, lips swollen. "I thought you wanted me to go slow?"

"And I want to fuck you."

Quinn undoes the button of her jeans and kicks them off. "Someone keeps changing his mind."

"Can you blame me when I have you?"

Mesmerized by the sight of her standing before me in a pair of orange lace underwear, I'm drooling. Before Quinn can remove them, I grab her hands to stop her.

"Let me."

Pressing kisses down her stomach, I kneel before her. I drag my nose along the wet fabric, inhaling her sweet scent.

Fuck, yeah, she is ready for me. There is no bigger

turn-on than seeing how wet I make her. Even from her doing a little strip tease for me.

"Jasper." She sinks her fingers into my hair as I lick over the material.

"I love how wet I make you. Are you fucking ready for me?"

"Yes."

"What do you want me to do?"

Her fingers tighten in my hair. "I thought you were deciding?"

"I am. But for right now, do you want me to fuck you or eat you out? It seems this little cunt of yours needs some relief."

"Eat me out. Please."

"Say it again."

"Please," she moans. "Please make me come, Jasper."

I slap her ass, listening to her gasp. "You're going to come on my tongue like the good girl that you are. Then you're going to come on my cock."

"Yes."

I waste no more time, sliding the fabric to the side and swiping my tongue through her wet folds.

So damn good. She tastes so damn good, I have to breathe through it so I don't come in my pants.

I strum her clit with my finger, then lick up every drop of wetness she gives me. Her pussy flutters around me as she gets close. I wrap one arm around her waist, feeling her body shake against me.

"Jasper, I…"

"That's right. Fucking come all over me."

It doesn't take more than a few licks before her release comes. I take everything she's giving me. By the time I pull back, my chin and mouth are wet and I have to rest her on the bed. She is completely sated, looking fucking sexy as hell lying there.

My hands roam over her body. Exploring. Tender touches. Letting her know how much I love her.

Love getting to do *this* to her.

"You ready for more?"

She peeks one eye open. "Yes."

Standing, I shed all of my clothes and watch as she licks her lips when my cock springs free.

"You want a taste?"

She nods.

Pressing one knee onto the bed, I feed her just the tip. Watching it disappear inside her pretty little mouth is heaven and hell all at once. It feels fucking amazing, but I'd rather be balls deep inside her pussy.

"Fuck, that feels amazing, Quinn."

She keeps going, sucking more in greedy slurps and pulls. Her mouth stretches around me to accommodate my size. She squeezes my balls and that about does me in.

"On your hands and knees," I command.

Flipping over to do just that, she shakes her ass at me.

Fuck. It is so perfect I can't help slapping it, marking it as mine. Her gasp has me sliding my dick through her cheeks.

"So fucking perfect, Quinn."

I rest my weight over her, kissing every inch of skin. I nibble on her shoulder, licking the sting away as her gasps and moans hit my ears.

"More of that."

"Want everyone to know who you belong to?" I ask, biting her again.

"I'm yours."

Reaching around, I finger her clit as I slide into her in one hard push.

"Jasper!"

Her cunt flutters and squeezes around me.

"I love how I make you feel." I press a kiss to her shoulder. "How easily you take me."

"It's like you were made for me."

"Damn fucking right."

I pull back, thrusting back inside. Her ass shakes as I quicken my movements. She's dripping as I pull out and push back in. I can't help but watch as she sucks me in every time.

"Faster, Jasper. Harder."

I give Quinn exactly what she wants. Holding on tight, I jack my hips and push inside her. She reaches out to hold on to the headboard as I move hard and fast. Sweat trickles down my abs as I growl at how tight she's squeezing me.

"Fuck, Quinn. I'm close. I need you to come."

My moves falter. I could explode now, but I want to feel her milk everything from me.

"Ah!" she shouts, burying her face in the pillow as her walls tighten around me.

"Thank fuck."

I keep thrusting, taking only a few more pumps before my balls draw up tight and I'm exploding inside her.

I nearly black out at how fucking good the orgasm feels rocking through me. I'm holding on to her, needing to stay grounded. My breaths are shallow as I pull out of her.

Watching my cum drip out of her? Best fucking sight in the world.

Before I can get up to clean her up, she's pulling me down and cuddling into my side. "Not yet. I need you."

"Are you okay?" A moment of panic hits me before she nods her head.

"I'm perfect. I just don't want you to go." She drops a kiss on my lips and pulls me close, chest to chest.

I wrap an arm around her and pull her closer as her fingers drag along my back.

"Trust me, Quinn. I'm not going anywhere."

"I know."

"Good. You might get sick of me."

She laughs into my side, her breath warm as my breathing evens out. "Never. That will never happen."

I hope she is right, because as long as I get to be with her in every way, I will be the happiest man on the planet.

Bar none.

Chapter Twenty-Six

JASPER

BODE

YOU'RE DATING GENEVIEVE?!

BODE

What the fuck man?

BODE

Why didn't you tell us?

BODE

I'm hurt

BODE

Forget the fact that she's a pop star

BODE

You're dating someone and didn't tell us?!

BODE

HOW RUDE

JASPER

Who told you?

NOAH

It might have slipped out

Might have?

GRAHAM

In his defense, he said you were dating someone

DAX

And did a terrible job of covering it up

MARCUS

Only because I have super dad hearing

MARCUS

I can't believe you're dating someone

MARCUS

How'd you meet her?

MARCUS

Is she good to you?

BODE

Way to be a dad, Cap

BODE

I still can't believe you didn't tell us

Would you have believed me?

BODE

No

BODE

Only because who would fall for your grumpy ass?!

See if I let you meet Quinn

BODE

I thought her name was Genevieve

It's her middle name

Quinn is her real name

BODE

I am learning so much

DAX

I would like to point out I did not tell anyone
while we were on the road

BODE

I'm still mad at you

BODE

You're my roomie and you didn't tell me?!

MARCUS

It's not Dax's news to tell

DAX

Exactly

NOAH

Oh, now you're agreeing with him, Dax?

NOAH

You were mad at me because I didn't tell
you either!

BODE

I can't believe everyone knew and didn't
tell us

MARCUS

Were you already dating her when we
offered to set you up?

Yes

MARCUS

Damn

MARCUS

You really couldn't have told us?

Again, would you have believed me?

DAX

I only believed him because I met her

MARCUS

Was she nice?

DAX

Very

NOAH

I like her

BODE

That's a rave review coming from you

NOAH

Asshole

BODE

When do I get to meet her?

Maybe if you're nice, you can come over later tonight

BODE

Seriously?

BODE

This seems too easy

Quinn suggested it

She wants to meet you guys

BODE

Obviously we'll be her favorite people

NOAH

Hey, I've already earned that title

DAX

Pretty sure Jasper has that title

It's true. She's my number one fan

BODE

My mind is still blown

MARCUS

BODE

For real though

If you can unblow your mind, come over to my place at seven tonight

BODE

Do the girls get to come?

Yes

DAX

Can we tell them ahead of time?

MARCUS

So they don't freak out of course

BODE

Hell, I might freak out

BODE

But that might be more reserved for Jasper than anyone else

Yes, you can tell them

BODE

We'll be there at seven then

See you then

BODE

I might come early and kick your ass first, Hayes

"You're on my ice now, Bella."

Quinn snickers. "How long have you been wanting to say that?"

"Oh, since we decided to go skating together."

I help her tie her skates so they're secure. She told me she's never done this, so I want to make sure she is ready to go. Even if she never wants to try it again, I want her to at least have fun today.

"You're way too excited for this," she says.

"Teaching the woman I love how to skate? You're fucking right I'm excited for it."

"You know I will probably be terrible, right?"

Quinn stands, her feet wobbling underneath her. I grasp her by the elbows and lead her onto the ice as she clutches onto my forearms.

"I won't let you fall, Quinn."

"I know."

"I'm going to start you off easy."

"How do I do this?" she asks, squeezing onto me even tighter.

"You'll want to find your balance. Bend your knees and stick your arms straight out in front of you."

Given that I'm still holding on to her, she only bends her knees. "Like this?"

"Yes. I'm going to let go so you can work on

balancing."

"Okay." She nods as I step away. Her arms stick straight out. "It's a good thing I don't have any shows because I am going to feel this in my core."

"Save those high notes for later, Bella." I start humming the tune to "Wildflowers in the Weeds."

"Jasper Hayes. Have you been listening to my music?"

"I told you I was going to."

"You like the upbeat ones?"

I shrug a shoulder as I watch her working on her balance.

"What can I say? It hooked me."

"Don't let the guys hear you say that." She laughs.

"Oh, I've already gotten enough shit from them, and I'll get even more tonight."

"At least you won't have to deal with it alone."

I smile back at her. "Is this why people decide to be in relationships? To get shit heaped on them together?"

"That and learning how to skate together."

"Well, you actually need to learn. Do you feel okay?"

She nods. "Yes."

"Good. You're a quick study. Now, what I want you to do is march. We can do it along the boards, so if you feel unsteady, you can grab on. But it'll help you get the feel of the ice under your skates."

"Okay."

A look of sheer concentration locks into place as she adjusts her position to start marching.

"You're doing good. Keep doing that."

"I feel dumb."

"Everyone starts somewhere."

Her eyes dart to mine before focusing back on the ice in front of her. "I bet you were a natural."

"Not everyone can be me." I wink at her.

"Yeah, yeah."

"You look good though, Quinn."

"You're just saying that."

I skate next to her. "Would I lie to you?"

"No."

"See? Want to try going out even farther onto the ice?"

"Will you catch me?" she asks.

"I won't need to, but yes. I won't let you fall."

"Just making sure."

Grabbing her hands, I pull her out toward the center of the rink. The Knights logo is painted underneath us.

"I want you to keep doing the marching. But every few feet, glide. Just keep those knees bent and you've got this."

Skating backward, I'm within arm's reach of her.

"Shouldn't you be paying attention to where you're going?"

I shake my head. "I know this ice like the back of my hand."

The rink is quiet. During practice earlier, I asked Coach Andrews if I could get a few extra hours on the ice. Being out here with Quinn is the perfect way to spend the afternoon. She is able to calm all the voices around me. The fans that never seem to shut their mouths—yelling that I'm too old and washed up to play.

None of that matters when I'm with her. Breathing in the cold air, it settles in my lungs.

"Next thing you know, you're going to be taking my job."

"March, march, glide," she repeats. "I don't know if I'll be playing hockey if I have to tell myself how to skate."

"We can come back if you want. Let you get your legs under you. Then you can skate circles around me."

"Definitely around Noah."

I burst out laughing, skating around her. "Fuck, that's my girl."

I start giving her more space on the ice, and soon Quinn is gliding more than marching. I don't say anything because I don't want to startle her, but she looks great out here.

I never thought it'd be such a turn-on to get to do the thing you love with the woman you love, but it is.

I fucking love it.

"Jasper! I'm doing it!"

She turns to look at me, but does it too quickly. Before she can fall, I'm catching her under her arms.

"Easy there, tiger."

"Got a little too cocky," she says.

"You looked great. We should come back and do this again."

"Only if we can go to karaoke again."

"At least you're a better skater than I am a singer."

"I happen to like your singing very much."

She smiles up at me. A knit Knights hat covers her head. Pink creeps up her cheeks from the cold. She looks fucking adorable.

Leaning down, I cover her mouth with mine.

"Now I know you're lying." I shake my head. "Want to go longer, or are you done?"

"My legs are burning, so I say we call it."

"Your choice."

"Besides, we should get back so we can start dinner."

I pull her back toward the bench. Kneeling before her, I start to untie her skates.

"Yes, I'd hate for us not to be able to make Brussels sprouts for everyone."

She grasps my chin and pulls my gaze to hers. "One of these days, Hayes, you'll learn to love them."

"Only for you, Quinn. Only for you."

Because if someone could make me love those wretched things, it's Quinn.

She makes loving anything easy. Because it's so easy to love her.

Chapter Twenty-Seven

"When are they getting here?" I arrange the last of the dishes on the counter.

"Should be any minute," Jasper says. "Are you nervous?"

"Honestly? No. Having met the other guys, I know I'll like them."

"My only hope is Bode behaves." Jasper laughs.

"He'll be fine."

"It's weird you already know all of them."

"Well, I don't *know them* know them," I say. "I only know them from playing. And that doesn't really count."

A knock sounds on the door. Jasper gives me a quick kiss before heading over and opening it. His face drops immediately.

"You brought Caleb?" Jasper asks, beckoning them in. "I thought it was adults only?"

"It's my Gran's night out and our babysitter was sick. I didn't want to miss tonight, so I figured you wouldn't mind. He's already been fed."

"I wasn't worrying about him eating Brussels sprouts," Jasper mutters.

"It's fine," I say. "I love babies."

"See? Quinn likes him," Bode goads. "Besides, I get a pass because you didn't tell me you were dating anyone."

"I told you not to bring that up," his girlfriend says. "I swear, we can't take them anywhere."

I smile at her. "I'm Quinn, and I can tell I'm going to like you a lot."

She blushes. "I'm Stevie. I'm just going to get this out of the way now and say I love your music. It's a shame what you're going through."

"I appreciate the vote of support."

"I would have punched that guy," she says. She tucks a curly lock of brown hair behind her ear.

"You and everyone else." I laugh. "Can I get you something to drink?"

She holds up a bottle of wine. "I brought some if you want a glass?"

"I'd love one."

Beer, wine, cocktails. I'm not picky when it comes to breaking the ice with Jasper's teammates and their partners.

A knock sounds again and Jasper is even more exacerbated when he answers it. "I apparently missed when I said it was kids' night."

Marcus and Harper arrive with their toddler, Dax and Chloe hot on their heels.

"The girls have play practice tonight and we didn't want to leave him with my mom since she had Bunco tonight. We couldn't find anyone on short notice."

"As long as he doesn't bother Zucchini," Jasper says. "I love your kids, but this is Zucchini's pad."

All the guys burst out laughing and I can't help but join in.

"Hey, don't give my Twatopotamus shit," Noah says, coming in before the door can close. "She's the best."

Everyone piles into the tiny condo. With this many people and two toddlers running around, it's cramped.

But I wouldn't want it any other way.

"Alright, let's get this done with," Jasper says, coming to stand next to me. "Everyone, I want you to officially meet Quinn, my girlfriend."

"About damn time," Bode calls out. "I was worried he was going to die alone."

"See? They love you," I whisper to Jasper.

"I guess." He kisses the top of my head before offering everyone drinks—kids included.

"I am so excited to meet you. I'm Harper." The blonde bombshell that arrived with Marcus sticks her hand out. "I promise, I'm usually very cool, but I might not be tonight."

I smile back at her as the last woman in the room comes over. "And I'm Chloe, but I'm guessing you already knew that. I can't believe I didn't recognize you at the shop. Who knew wearing a hat could work as a disguise?"

"I love your rings," I gush, holding my hand out to her. "This ring? I'm obsessed with it."

The other girls hold out their hands with matching rings with the crossed hockey sticks. "We are too. Chloe is so talented," Harper says.

"Seriously. I wish I had that much talent," Stevie says.

"Stop it." Chloe blushes furiously. "I should be gushing over you."

I wave her off. "Please. I can't imagine how much goes into making each ring."

"I've had to hire a few more people to help because of

you," she points out. "I can't tell you what it meant to me that you came to the store."

"I would have been there opening night if people knew Jasper and I were together."

"Dax said you two met online?" Chloe asks.

I eye Jasper over them. His gaze is locked on mine as he chats with the guys.

It's nights like this that I can't wait to have in the future. I don't know what tomorrow holds at this moment. If I'll be able to go on tour again and record more music. The future is murky. With Jasper talking about retiring, our careers are both up in the air. But at least we have each other to help us wade through the unknown.

"Yeah. I don't know how we matched, but he made a cat joke and I was a goner."

"You must be special if Jasper kept you to himself for this long," Harper says.

I smile at her. "He's a pretty special guy himself."

"I know the guys worried about him," Stevie says. "They thought he was lonely."

"I've felt that way sometimes."

"We all have," Stevie agrees. "I had my fair share of bad exes. I got lucky finding Bode."

A lovesick look comes over her. No doubt the same one I have when thinking about Jasper.

"We're all lucky," Harper says.

"You ladies ready to eat?" Bode comes up behind us, wrapping Stevie in his arms.

"Hmm, I guess so." Stevie presses up onto her toes to kiss Bode. He looks just as lovesick as she does.

It'd be hard to watch if I didn't have that with Jasper.

"How's it going?" He pulls me off to the side as everyone starts to serve themselves.

"Good. I really like them."

"I knew you would. They're good people."

Jasper takes Caleb from Noah so he can make a plate.

"This guy is a cutie," I say, waggling my fingers in front of him. He lights up.

"He is. Let's hope he doesn't take after his dad." Jasper laughs.

"I heard that, you jerk."

"Jerk? Watch it, Bode. That one hit below the belt." Jasper feigns hurt.

"I can't cuss in front of Caleb. He's repeating everything we say. I don't need him to tell his nanny to eff off."

Caleb repeats jerk a few times and I laugh at how cute he is.

"See?" Bode jabs the serving spoon at us. "I have to set a good example for my kid."

"Do you want kids?" Jasper asks. "I know this is something we probably should have talked about before tonight, but hey, I'm asking now."

"If we get lucky."

Jasper pulls me into his arms. "Quinn, I'm already the luckiest guy on the earth because I have you."

Swoon.

I love this man and how he has no problem showing me how he feels.

"Well, if we get lucky enough to have one, then we'll have one."

The thought of Jasper with our kids? Teaching them to skate? Watching our favorite Julie Andrews movies? Loving cereal and hating vegetables?

I would give up every future imaginable in singing to have that with Jasper.

"You want to hold him?" Jasper asks.

"Sure."

I take him and head over to the table where Stevie sets up a portable booster seat for him. The guys head over to the living room to sit and eat.

"He likes you," Stevie says.

Caleb is smiling at me as he stares up at me.

"He's cute."

"Thanks," Stevie says. "Let me get him settled so we can eat."

"Do you want me to grab him a plate?" I ask.

"I'll take care of it. He's starting to get picky about what he's eating."

"I feel that," Harper says. "We still struggle to get Jamie to eat anything green."

"I do not envy you," I say.

"I hope if we have another, they're as good as Caleb," Stevie says.

"He is the best baby," Chloe agrees. "If I wasn't so busy with the store, we might consider having one."

I wish that were my biggest concern right now. The trial is going to be here in a few weeks. It's all I can do not to focus on it.

Making music is not cheap. Studio time. Production. Tours. It costs a lot. Something Eric drilled into my head. If none of that money gets recovered, it's going to be damn hard to start over.

"You know, I'm having the girls over to watch the game next week. Do you want to come?" Chloe asks, interrupting me from my thoughts.

"I'd love to."

It'll be a good distraction for me. That and I think I like the idea of making friends with these women.

I have a feeling they'll be in my life for a long time. I

don't know how much longer Jasper will be playing, but even if he retires, these guys are like family, and I feel like I could have the same bond with them as Jasper has with his teammates.

Because this thing with Jasper? I plan on it lasting forever.

Chapter Twenty-Eight

JASPER

"**A**re you ready to get back out there?" Marcus asks.

"Fuck, yeah," I say.

"Shoulder feeling good?"

"Feels great." I give it a roll for good measure. "Trust me, I wouldn't be back if I wasn't ready.

"Good. We need you out there," Bode agrees. "We've got a tough road ahead of us if we're going to make the playoffs."

"We're looking good though," Noah says, rapping his knuckles against his chair. "If only it was a home game tonight to welcome you back, Jasper."

"I'm just glad to be back on the ice."

Especially since San Jose is a tough opponent. They're in the running for the top seed in the western conference. Analysts are calling it a preview of the finals.

No pressure, right?

"Alright, men. We've got a tough game ahead of us tonight." Coach Andrews calls our attention to him. "Having Jasper back is going to make a big difference."

Whoops and cheers greet me, and fuck, it feels good. It feels nice to be wanted by the team.

"San Jose is a good team. Let's stick to the game plan and we've got a shot to bring home the win."

By the time we're walking out to start the game, Noah is bumping his elbow against mine. "We've got this."

"Yeah, we do."

"Going to have the game of our lives."

"Damn straight," I agree. "Let's show these young kids how the game is played."

The game starts off on a high note. Everyone is skating well. Marcus and Bode start off strong but don't get any points on the board before Noah and I start our shift.

It's easy to read one another. Where he is, I'm there. Wherever the puck is, it's like my stick is a magnet for it.

Getting my legs under me in a game feels pretty damn good.

It's like whatever we do out here, we can't be stopped. Before our shift ends, I put the puck in the back of the net.

"Fuck, yeah!" I skate behind the net, pumping my fists in the air.

"That was amazing!" Noah jumps on top of me. "Fucking amazing!"

"Felt damn good."

"Great job!" Coach Andrews claps me on the helmet as we make our way back to the bench. "I like what I'm seeing out there."

We keep the momentum going. It's like the one goal was the fuel we needed to add more points to the board. Bode gets an easy one in, followed by Marcus. Damn. Up 3-0 before the end of the first? It's about as fun of a game as they get.

Graham looks good as he starts his shift for the second period and adds another goal. It's like we can do no wrong.

We're stopping every shot they have on goal. Nothing gets close to our net. It's the kind of play that we'll be studying for years—it's *that* flawless. It's like we're a completely different team from when we played Dallas. We're on fire tonight.

Another goal puts us up 5-0 before the end of the second.

"Gentlemen. You're on fire, but I don't want you to settle." Coach Andrews claps as we wait out the intermission before starting the third. "Our defense looks good. That's what I want to see. Keep that up."

That's exactly what we do. San Jose is fighting hard. Our goalie keeps knocking the puck away or snatching them right out of the air with his glove.

"Damn. He's crushing it tonight," Noah says next to me on the bench.

"I'm glad he's on our team."

The two of us are called up and we hop over the boards and get moving. My skates dig into the ice as I move toward our zone. The puck sails into my stick and I fly down the ice. I dodge one of their defensemen—thank God, because the last thing I want is to aggravate my shoulder—and send the puck to our winger.

Our winger is on a breakaway. He dekes out the goalie and puts the biscuit in the net.

"Hell, yeah!" I go over to congratulate him.

"Way to set me up." He slaps me on the helmet.

"All you," I say.

Boos rain down on us from the home crowd as we skate back to the bench. In the middle of the third, there's no way they're going to be able to come back from this.

San Jose is able to get the puck in the net when they pull their goalie, ending the game 6-1.

We shake hands with them on the ice, and are met with the standard reporters in the locker room after.

"Jasper. How do you think you did out there tonight?"

Based on his microphone, he's from one of the local stations.

"I felt pretty good. I'm glad I was able to help contribute to the team's win and putting us one step closer to securing a playoff position."

"Do you think you'll get a lot of ice time if you make the playoffs?"

I grind my teeth, trying not to let him bother me. "All I know is I had a good game tonight, and I hope I can keep playing well to help my team keep winning games."

"And if Coach Andrews decides not to play you?" he asks.

"Then that's a question you'll need to ask Coach Andrews. Thanks."

I end the interview before he can keep asking me inane questions.

This is one of the things I dislike most about hockey. No matter how well you play, it's always how can you play better? Considering my age and coming back from an injury, I thought I played fucking phenomenal tonight. It dampens my spirits as I head back to the locker room. I barely hear a word of Coach's postgame speech, accepting a few claps on the back before I hit the showers.

We've got a long road trip coming up. Instead of going home to Quinn, we're getting on the bus to head back to the hotel. At least I should be able to video chat with her.

"Hey, man, don't listen to those guys," Marcus says as we head out of the arena toward the bus. "You looked great out there tonight. That's all that counts."

"I mean, what is it going to take to impress these guys?

Two hat tricks? Seven assists? Maybe pulling the Stanley Cup out of my ass to hoist?"

"Okay, that's a little much," Bode says, coming up on my other side. "Why don't we grab some beers and decompress when we get back to the hotel?"

"I don't know. I was kind of hoping to call Quinn."

Bode laughs, showing me his phone. "They're all still out."

Quinn, Stevie, Chloe, and Harper are all at Chloe's, watching the game. I love that they invited her to hang out with them. Being in the spotlight, it's hard for her to make friends. They welcomed her with open arms.

"Damn. I guess we do have time for a drink."

"We're going upstairs," Noah says.

"Yeah, we're tired." Graham waves goodbye to us as they head to the elevator.

I snort. "Tired, my ass."

"Well, we can grab a drink and then head up," Bode says. "I'm sure the girls will be home by then."

"I'm glad they included Quinn," I say.

Marcus heads to the bar to order a pitcher of beer as we grab a table.

"Stevie really liked her. I mean, she won over Caleb, and that wins me over."

"Doesn't take much for you." I laugh.

"Hey, if my kid likes you, that's how I judge a person now."

"Well, I'm glad you both do."

"Things seem to be going well," Dax comments.

"Really well," I confirm.

"You know, we might give you grief," Bode starts, "but we do it because we love you, man."

"I know." I smile at him as Marcus arrives back at the table and hands a glass to everyone.

"And even though I'm still kind of mad you lied to us—"

"He didn't lie," Dax interrupts. "Technically he just didn't tell us."

"I'm happy you're happy," Bode finishes, ignoring Dax.

"Thanks, man. I am happy."

"We can tell," Marcus says. "Even though you begrudgingly had us over, it was nice for all of us to be together."

"Hey." I point a finger at him. "It was not begrudgingly. There was no grudging."

"Who knew all it would take for you to like us is for you to date a pop star?" Bode laughs.

"I liked you before." I roll my eyes. "Now? Not so much."

"I see how it is." Bode flips me off. "We're chopped liver now that you have Quinn."

"And Zucchini. Don't forget about Zucchini." I give him a cheesy smile.

"Wait until you get a kid," Bode says. "They're the best."

"One thing at a time," I tell him.

I smile at all the guys. Bode pulls out his phone to show us new pictures of Caleb that we haven't seen. Marcus counters with more pictures of his kids.

It's hard to imagine this is how we are now. Back in the early days, we'd close down the bars. I'd have a short relationship here and there—casual on both sides.

Now? All of us are in serious relationships.

"Can I make a toast?" I ask.

"Floor is yours," Marcus says, waving his hand in front of him.

"I know we've all had our ups and downs over the years and that life has thrown us a lot of curveballs, but

I'm glad all of you are by my side. I don't have much in the way of family, but you guys have become that to me and have always had my back. So thank you. I love you guys."

"We love you, man," Bode says.

"Yeah, ditto," Dax agrees.

Marcus laughs. "Yeah. We've got your back. We love you, Jasper."

"Thanks."

It's on the tip of my tongue to tell them I'm debating about retiring, but I don't want to. There's still too much unknown heading into the playoffs. I don't want it to be a distraction. I want our entire focus to be on making the playoffs and how far we can go.

There will be plenty of time to talk futures.

At least there is one certain.

Quinn.

The only certainty in my life that I need.

Chapter Twenty-Nine

QUINN

"Thanks for coming in today," Rebecca says, offering me a seat at the oversized conference room table. "How are you feeling?"

I shake my head back and forth. "Nervous."

"That's to be expected with our court date next week."

I set my bag down next to me and twiddle my thumbs in my lap. "Any updates?"

"Our forensic accountant thinks he might be onto something."

"Really?" I try not to get my hopes up, but this is a large part of my worries. If they can't find the money Eric stole, how are they going to prove he did it and not someone else?

"He's still working on it, and I don't know if it's going to pan out, but I wanted to tell you he *might* have something."

"Okay." I blow out a breath.

With Jasper in the middle of a road trip, it sucks that I don't have him with me every night. Talking on the phone with him and texting isn't the same thing as having him next to me.

"We have a strong case," Rebecca says, sliding over a stack of paper. "I want you to review the facts of everything so they're fresh in your mind. And this is what we know. They're facts. No matter how Eric's attorney tries to twist the truth, I want you to be confident in knowing you know the truth."

"Easier said than done."

I open the folder and look over the first page.

"You're a pop star, Genevieve. You perform on stage for thousands of people. You've got this."

"Yeah, but having to be in the same room as my ex? I don't know."

The nerves about the trial have been simmering for the last two weeks. This date has been fixed in my mind for the last few months. Jasper has been the best distraction, but now that he's gone, it's hard to keep a clear head.

"Is there anything I can do to help?" Rebecca asks, coming around the table.

"What if we lose? What if Eric goes in there and sweet-talks them and I come out with nothing? I don't know how I'm going to start over."

"We'll worry about that *if* it happens. There's no point in counting your losses before they happen. Besides"—she brushes her hair behind her shoulder—"I happen to be very good at my job and don't plan on losing."

I give her a weak smile. "I appreciate your confidence."

"I'll give you some of it. We have a strong case, and *if*"—again, I appreciate her saying if, not when—"anything bad happens, you still have a small amount of money set aside that you can use to produce a new album."

"But touring is expensive."

"And you're the biggest pop star in the world. You

haven't released a new album in two years. People will eat it up. Have faith that it is all going to work out."

"Faith. Right." I suck in a deep breath, rolling that over in my head. "It's hard to have that when I'm worried about finding a new manager that won't fuck me over."

She pats my hand. "That's why you'll have me vet them. We'll do a deep dive into whoever you want and make sure they're on the up and up."

"At least I have a good lawyer on my team."

"Damn straight. Now, I'm going to let you review everything and come check on you in a little bit. Let me know if you have any questions. It's everything you've told me, so again, all facts."

"All facts."

"You'll do great on the stand."

I give her a nod as she leaves me to it.

Instead of going through the papers, I fish my phone out of my bag.

JASPER

How's the meeting going?

QUINN

Okay

Okay good or okay bad?

Okay fine

Just reviewing everything I've told her

They might have a lead on the money

Really? That's promising

It also might be nothing

Could be something

I don't want to get my hopes up

Mind if I keep my hopes up for you then?

I know it's going to work out for you

You're awfully positive today

The world deserves your music, Quinn

I refuse to believe anything else

MY HEART SWELLS at Jasper's words. This is why I wish he were here. He's about the only person in the world that knows what to say to keep me from spiraling.

I love you

And I really hate that you're on this road trip right now

I love you too

I'll be home in time for court

You're sure you want to come?

You couldn't pay me enough to keep me away

Good, because I don't have that much money 😛

You will next week

I've got to run

Practice

Keep me posted on how the rest of the meeting goes

I will

♥

WITH JASPER'S messages in my mind, it's easier to review all the documents at hand. Seeing what I pulled in financially and what I actually made stokes the fire in my belly.

What an asshole I signed with. I know he has a few other clients, but after Rebecca talked to them, none of them reported anything nefarious.

Just me. He only saw fit to steal *from me*. I hope that Rebecca's accountant can find something so we can put Eric away. Preying on my hopes and dreams? He's the lowest of the low.

I can't believe I let myself fall for him. He said all the right things. Promised me the world.

Turns out, I don't need the world.

I want my music. I want to perform. Whether that's on a world stage or in a karaoke booth for one person, I'll be okay with it.

Because as long as I have a hockey player and a few cats to come home to?

I'll be happy.

Chapter Thirty

JASPER

Fuck.

Walking out of the hotel to catch the bus to the rink, a heavy wet snow is falling. At least two inches coats the sidewalk.

Not good.

We're supposed to leave Denver tonight after our game and head back to Nashville. With Quinn's trial tomorrow, getting stuck here is the very last thing I need.

Not that I should even be thinking that, but it's a sticky snow and I'm worried.

"Think it'll clear up by tonight?" I ask Noah, dropping down into the seat across from him.

He taps on his phone and holds it up for me to see. "They're predicting at least eight inches."

"Fuck."

"If we can't leave tonight, we'll head home tomorrow."

"That's not what I'm worried about," I say, passing his phone back.

"What's the issue?"

I drop my voice, turning my head from side to side to make sure no one is listening. "Quinn's trial starts tomorrow."

"Oh, shit," he mutters. "And you were going to be there?"

I nod. "I was planning on it."

I realize it's pointless to keep my voice down because showing up in court tomorrow is going to announce to the world that the two of us are together. I mean, why else would a hockey star be at her trial?

"Denver is used to this kind of weather. I don't think it'll be an issue."

"Knock on wood." I rap my knuckles against the back of the seat in front of me.

"Not actually wood," Bode points out, turning around.

"Not the point," I hiss.

"Just worry about the game and then you can worry about the weather," Bode reiterates. "Nothing else you can do now."

"Easy for you to say."

The drive to the arena is a slow crawl. Between the weather and the traffic downtown, it does nothing to soothe my nerves.

I would give anything to be back home with Quinn right now. Hockey schedules are not forgiving when you would rather be anywhere else.

It feels like I'm letting her down by not being there with her. I've done my best to keep a positive attitude with her, but I still worry about what might happen if that fucker gets off scot-free.

It would devastate Quinn.

But I can't think about that.

Not as the bus finally pulls into the arena.

I push myself harder during practice and warm-ups than necessary. The burn in my legs helps quiet the thoughts racing through my head.

What I'm doing here? Not as important as Quinn.

All I've ever wanted in my life is to have something to show for it. That I've accomplished something.

Playing for a winless team for so long and not having anyone to come home to? Being one of the least liked players on the team? Never a fun feeling.

All of that changed when Quinn came walking—well, more like messaging—into my life. Thank God I didn't scare her away with that feline connection joke.

She's all that matters now. As much as I would love to lift the Cup above my head, she's the most important thing.

And I hate that I'm not there for her when she needs me the most.

"You good, man?" Graham asks as we head out to the tunnel for the puck drop to start the game.

"I'm good." I nod, blowing out a breath.

Hockey. I can't think about anything else.

With a win tonight, we can lock up a playoff spot. That's all I need to worry about. Knowing Quinn is watching—and will be pissed if we lose—carries me through the start of the game.

Hopping over the boards to start my shift, I do everything I can to keep the momentum for the Knights up. Noah and I are skating well together, keeping the Black Diamonds off the board. Their goalie is one of the best in the league, but Bode is better, capitalizing on a missed pass.

Marcus chirps with Hollins, a friend of his from college, after the goal. Even though it's 1-0, they won't let the game get too far ahead of them.

That's exactly what they do. They tie up the game before the second period, and take the lead with an easy goal at the start of the period from Cash Williams, one of their stars who also happens to be married to Noah's sister.

Noah stops a goal from going in by taking one to the pads, and I'm able to grab the rebound and take off down the ice. Our winger is right there with me and I fire it over to him to tie up the game.

Fuck, yeah.

This is exactly what I need. We're skating hard and giving Colorado a run for their money.

They are always one of the best teams in the league, and it feels fucking amazing to be tied with them right now.

Marcus and Bode take the ice, and watching the two of them play together is a thing of beauty. The way they read each other on the ice? It's only something you can learn from playing together for so long.

We end the second period tied at 2-2 but come out swinging in the third. They aren't ready for us and we get two easy goals to pull ahead.

They get another goal halfway through the third, but we're able to fend off their advances to close out the game 4-3.

"Playoffs, baby!" Noah claps me on the helmet as we skate off the ice. "I'll never get used to this feeling."

"Feels pretty damn good," I say, meaning it.

Because even though hockey isn't the most important thing in my life anymore, it still feels amazing.

"Great goal tonight," Graham congratulates me as we head into the locker room.

"Thanks, man. Their goalie was caught off guard."

Graham shakes his head, tossing his gear into his stall.

"Doesn't matter. A goal is a goal and without it, we wouldn't have locked up the playoff spot."

"He's right," Bode agrees. "We need to celebrate when we get home."

"Sorry, men. Looks like we're not getting out tonight," Coach Andrews says as we all gather around him post-shower.

"Fuck." I bang my head against the back of the locker. "Fuck, fuck, fuck."

"Anything we can do to help?" Marcus asks.

"Assuming Noah filled you in then?" I turn to look at him.

"Yeah. Sorry, man. Not ideal but you want to get home in one piece."

"I know. I'm going to call Quinn when we get back to the hotel."

Marcus claps me on the shoulder. "I'll get these guys down to the bar so you can have some peace and quiet."

"Thanks, man."

I pull out my phone to text her, but like after every game, a message is waiting for me.

QUINN

PLAYOFFS!

Hell yeah!

I knew you could do it

You guys looked great out there

I can't wait to celebrate when you get home
tonight

FUCK. I hate the sick feeling that washes over me because I won't be there for her. Forget about me, it's her I'm worried about.

JASPER

About that...

QUINN

Is everything okay?

We're grounded tonight

Too much snow

Fuck

Do you know when you'll leave?

No clue

I haven't left the arena yet, so I'm not sure how much snow has come down since we got here

It's okay

No it's not

What if I don't get back in time?

I'll manage

You shouldn't have to

Claire said she'd be there too

I have her

I know

But I want to be there for you

I hate snow

Can I personally petition the NHL
commissioner so you never have to play a
team in a cold weather city during the
winter?

That's just what I needed

Doubtful, but if anyone could, it'd be you

It's just rude you can't get home

What if I were having a baby and you
needed to get home?

Well, we'd be royally fucked then

Because I plan on getting home in one
piece to you

Ugh!

Stupid snow

It'll be okay

Claire will be there for you

Eric will get what's coming to him

And when the season is over, you and I are
going to take a vacation together

Switzerland?

I hear the beer there is amazing

Throw in some fondue, and I'm sold

I love you

I love you too

Don't worry about me

Focus on tomorrow and kicking his ass

Ass-kicking mode locked in

I've got this

That's my girl

Chapter Thirty-One

QUINN

QUINN

Any updates on when you'll get here?

JASPER

No

Coach said maybe in the next few hours,
but nothing guaranteed

I was hoping it would've cleared out by now

Shouldn't Denver be used to this?

One would think

Why does it have to snow in Denver in
March?

It is still technically winter

I thought you were smart 😜

Har-har

Only doing it because I can't think about
you not being here today

I know, babe

I'm so sorry

I'd be there if I could

I know

Sometimes I hate our jobs

They're the fucking worst

But you know that I'll be there in spirit

I know 🩶

And we'll be able to celebrate when I get back

Let's not get ahead of ourselves

I know things are going to go well and you'll win

Knock on wood!

And when you do, dinner's on you 😶

And if I don't win?

Dinner's on me 😶

I love you, Jasper

I know

I love you too

I keep reading the texts with Jasper from this morning. Rebecca sent a car to pick me up so I wouldn't have to worry about any of the madness at the courthouse today. I smooth my hands down my tailored pants.

Black, wide-legged pants. White blouse with a ribbon tie at the top. Dark green blazer. I even picked out my pointiest heels to round out my suit of armor today. I'll need everything possible to feel in control.

It'd be easier if Jasper were here, but I can't think about that.

It's a cold, gray morning as I'm dropped off in front of the courthouse. Press is already lingering outside. Of course they are. I've made a point to ignore all the entertainment channels these last few months because I didn't want to hear what anyone was saying about the trial.

Questions are lobbed at me as I fight through the crowds pressing in on me.

"How are you feeling today, Genevieve?"
"Do you think you'll come out on top?"
"How will it feel to see your ex again?"
"Do you think you're being greedy?"

I DON'T SAY a word as I push through the doors to the courthouse. Warmth and the smell of old paper greets me as I spot Rebecca just beyond the security checkpoint.

Going through, the security officer gives me a nod as I grab my bag and make my way over to Rebecca.

"How are you feeling today?"

"Nervous."

She beams back at me. "Well, you might not need to be."

"What? What do you mean?"

Before she can answer, Eric comes sauntering in, a cocky look on his face. When he spots me, he shoots a wink my direction.

Everything about the asshole is smarmy. From that grin on his face to his slicked-back hair to the cheap suit he's wearing.

God, I can't wait to wipe that look off his face.

"I hate him," I mutter under my breath.

Rebecca's paralegal rushes over to us to beckon us into the courtroom. It's smaller than I imagined it would be as the old doors creak shut behind us. The state seal hangs behind the judge's bench, with a few rows of seats—packed with people—behind the small wall that separates us from them. The court reporter is waiting to the left of the bench, with no jury inside yet.

Eric is chatting with his attorney as we walk up the aisle.

"When will the jury arrive?" I ask Rebecca, taking my seat. Looking around, I see Claire in the front row, and she gives me a reassuring smile.

"We might not get to that today," she says, taking out her files and a manila envelope.

"Why not?" A sick feeling settles in my stomach.

Before she can answer, we're called to stand for the arriving judge.

"Your honor, I have new evidence I would like to submit to the court."

"You do?" I whisper.

She smiles down at me, nodding.

"Approach the bench."

She walks up with all the confidence in the world.

"What evidence is this? We weren't made aware of any evidence, Your Honor," Eric's attorney pipes up.

Rebecca aims a well-practiced smile his way. "We only discovered it late last night. It was couriered to your office this morning."

"We didn't receive it."

"I have a copy for you, then." She produces another file and passes it over as the judge starts to review everything in front of her.

What in the world is going on?

The old, wooden door creaks open. Sneaking a peek, I do a double take.

Jasper?

Based on the rumpled appearance of his suit, he came straight from the airport. My eyes track his. They scan the courtroom, looking for a seat. When he spots me, he winks at me and I can breathe.

No matter what happens now, I'm going to be okay.

The judge peers up over her glasses.

"Have you had a chance to review this yet, Mr. Taylor?"

"I..." Eric's attorney stutters, consulting with the man who looks white as a ghost.

Rebecca shoots me a quick look, and while things appear to be favoring me, I have no idea what is going on.

"We need more time to review the evidence presented." He clears his throat and straightens.

"It appears you do, as it looks like Miss Rose is not the only person who your client has stolen from."

"What?" I gasp, covering my mouth.

There's no way I heard her correctly. I'm not the only person he stole from? There were others? Rebecca said I was the only one.

"Our forensic accountant was able to uncover the

accounts to which Mr. Powers was laundering his money to."

Oh my God. I can't believe they found it.

"In doing so, he uncovered several other accounts that he stole from. While we are still working to determine who they are, there is clear evidence that he stole from Miss Rose."

I turn, eyes finding Claire and then Jasper. A huge grin sits on his face.

"In light of this new evidence, court will be adjourned and the bailiff will take Mr. Powers into custody pending a new trial on the counts of embezzlement and wire fraud."

She raps her gavel before ordering everyone to rise.

"I'm being framed!" Eric shouts as he's put into handcuffs. "I didn't do this."

The sight of him being led away in cuffs, shouting that he's being wronged, might be the best thing I'll see all year.

"When did you find this?" I ask Rebecca, wrapping her in a hug. Tears well in my eyes as I try to keep it together.

"Last night. We were working down to the wire and he got it. It's over, Quinn."

"I can't believe it. Is the money there?"

She waggles her head back and forth. "There's a good chunk, but it's hard to know whose is whose. It will take a while to unravel that thread, but you won."

"Yeah, she did!" Claire squeezes me from behind.

"Holy shit!" I cover my mouth as the floodgates open.

I spin on my heel, and Jasper is there to sweep me into his arms.

"You're here."

"Where else would I be?"

"Oh, I don't know. Stuck at a hotel in Denver?" I pull back, cupping his cheeks. "I can't believe you're here."

"We were able to get out early this morning. Came straight here."

"I think you might be my good luck charm." I kiss him. I don't care that the room is packed full with people. The only person that matters is Jasper.

That and the fact that this whole ordeal is going to be behind me. No question if he'll get off now. Eric is getting what he deserves, having taken advantage of not only me, but others as well.

The scumbag.

"Want to get out of here?" Jasper whispers against my lips, dropping his forehead to mine.

"More than anything."

I pull Claire in for a hug before she leaves. "Thank you for being here."

"Anything for you. Well, and to see that asshole go down."

"That image of him saying he was being framed will live rent free in my head for a long time."

"Same. Now, go enjoy your man."

I peer back at Jasper. "I will."

Jasper links hands with me as we all leave the courtroom.

"I'll be in touch as to next steps," Rebecca says. "There is going to be a lot of paperwork to sort through, but you're free of him."

I sink into Jasper's side, leaning on him to hold me up. "I still can't believe it."

"Believe it. You're free to do whatever you want. Record, tour, do nothing. All up to you."

"I mean, I know the money won't be coming soon, but wow. The idiot still has it."

"What a dumb fuck," Jasper mutters so only I can hear.

"I'll keep you posted." Rebecca pulls her phone out as she's waving goodbye. "Talk soon."

Jasper and I follow suit, walking out hand-in-hand into the still-gray morning. Flashbulbs are popping but we ignore them all as we head down to the waiting car.

"Genevieve. How do you feel now that you've won against your former manager?"
"What are you going to do next?"
"Any new music in the works?"
"Care to comment on your relationship?"

I IGNORE them all as Jasper swings open the door for me and I crawl in the backseat. More questions are shouted as he gets in and closes the door behind us.

I slide as close as possible to him, pulling him in for a long, drugging kiss.

Thank God for tinted windows.

"I still can't believe you made it."

"It was iffy there, but I've never been happier to see Nashville in my life."

"Thank you for being here for me, Jasper. I don't know if I would have made it without you these last few months."

He shakes his head. "You would have. You're the strongest person I know."

I squeeze him to me, burying my face in the scent of cedar and fresh laundry. "You're my center, Jasper. The only thing in my chaotic world that makes sense."

"You have me, Quinn. I will be by your side every single day. For the rest of our lives."

I smile against his neck. "As long as it doesn't snow in Denver."

Chapter Thirty-Two

"Thank you, Nashville! You've been amazing tonight."

Looking around, cheers echo around the intimate venue where I'm performing tonight. It's an out-of-body experience. The crowd, the lights, the music. Everything feels different. Better. *Euphoric.*

All evening, everyone has been singing along. I was so worried about tonight, having put it together on such short notice. By the time I came back out for the encore, every single person was on their feet.

"I can't tell you what this moment means to me."

It's my first show in over a year as more cheers ring out. Lights from phones and signs held up shine from the seats.

"It's been a long time since I've been in front of a crowd like this and to do it in front of my adopted home crowd? It's the best feeling in the world. I love all of you and I love this city." Glancing over to the side of the stage, even though I can't see him, I know exactly where Jasper is. Having just gotten back into town from a road game, we had little time together before the show tonight.

With the Knights heading to the playoffs, our lives are going to get even busier. It's why I decided to do one show here in Nashville to raise money for the team's charitable foundation. I mean, that's how Jasper and I met, so I figured it'd be the perfect way to get back into things.

Having signed with NASH—Nashville Artists Studio House—I've been able to start recording again. Who knew falling in love with the *right* person could make some damn good music? Better than anything I've done in the past.

"I want to thank you all again for coming out tonight. You sold this place out when I was worried none of you would show up." More raucous cheers. "Before I go and close out tonight, I want to debut a brand-new song for you. I've been keeping this one close to the vest. It's reminiscent of the journey I've gone through, and I thought tonight would be the perfect opportunity to debut it."

The crowd goes wild as the opening chords of "Plastic Smile" come on even though they've never heard the song.

It's only me on the stage. No backup singers and only a single spotlight shining down on me. I get lost in the words as I sing.

When I come to the first bridge, my voice wavers. No one but me would notice it. A broken heart. Shattered. Crushed.

It's something I haven't felt in a long time.

Because I feel safe. Loved.

The world can throw anything at me, but with Jasper, I can handle it.

When I get to the chorus again, the fans are already singing along. Emotion clogs my throat as I try to sing, but I can't.

I hold the mic out for them to sing and they respond in kind.

One time and they know the words. It's why I have

the best fans in the world and love getting to do this. They're supporting me as I get back to where I want to be.

Then you came walking in
Open arms, safe and sound
A place to land
The home I never had

TEARS ARE POURING down my face as I get to the part about falling back in love. I can't help it. I'm feeling everything tonight.

I lean into the music as I hit the final note. Opening my eyes, I look out and the crowd is going wild. It only makes more tears fall. Goose bumps break out on my skin at the excitement coursing through me.

"Thank you, Nashville!" I yell one more time before running off stage.

Jasper is waiting for me with open arms, tears in his eyes. All of our friends are waiting behind him, cheering me on.

"That was phenomenal. They loved you."

He sweeps me off my feet, spinning us around.

"I can't believe I got to do that."

"They loved you," Claire calls out.

"Fucking brilliant," Bode agrees.

"I have chills, Quinn. Chills," Chloe says. "You were incredible."

"Thanks, guys. I'm so glad you were here."

Over the last few weeks, I've gotten to know all of them well. We've been spending a lot of time together while the guys have been traveling for games. It's nice to not feel so alone in the world.

"Do you think you're ready for this every night?" I ask Jasper.

"Hitting the road with you? I'm ready."

"Wait, hitting the road? What are you talking about?" Noah asks.

Jasper groans, resting his forehead against mine. "Why does he always hear everything?"

"Because you don't whisper," Noah fires back. "What's going on?"

"Are you ready to tell them?" I ask.

Jasper tucks a lock of hair that escaped my bun behind my ear. "Yeah."

We turn to face them, and all eyes are on Jasper. Looping my arm through his, I give him a reassuring squeeze.

"I'm retiring," Jasper says evenly.

He's had his moments of wavering, but since he finally made the decision, he's at peace with it.

"You didn't discuss this with us," Bode says.

Marcus looks at Jasper and nods, like he knows it's time.

"I'm old," he says. "We all know it. I can't keep putting myself through this. Hockey has been my everything for most of my life, and it's about time someone else gets that attention."

"Aww. Jasper, I'm so happy for you." Harper comes over and gives him a hug. "The team won't be the same without you."

"You're not leaving before the playoffs, right?" Graham asks. "We need you."

"After the playoffs. No matter what happens, I'm

hanging up my skates. I'm hoping we can make a run for it."

Everyone knocks on wood and I bark out a laugh. I'm not going to tell them to change things now, because the team is looking good. While Jasper heads to the playoffs, I'm heading back to the recording studio. The court released part of the funds I'm owed from Eric, but the rest? It's going to take more time to sort out.

And I'm okay with it. The buzz for my new album is putting my old songs into the top one hundred again. It's helping with the cost of the tour this fall.

A smaller one here in the states before hitting Canada in the spring and Europe next summer.

Spending the summer with Jasper abroad? I can't think of anything better.

"You're not going to move away from Nashville, are you?" Dax asks. "That would really suck to lose you."

I shake my head. "We're not going anywhere. Nashville is home."

"Does that mean you're going to kick off your tour here?" Stevie asks, coming to my side and pulling me in for a hug.

"Damn right we are."

"We all better get tickets. I plan on going to every show we can," Claire says.

"Don't worry." I laugh. "You all will have VIP tickets whenever you want to come."

"Then I think this calls for a celebration," Marcus says. "Sin Bin?"

"For a little while," Jasper says.

"Man, you are getting old," Noah says. "You can't hang out even for a few hours?"

Bode smacks him in the head. "You realize we have practice in the morning, right?"

The guys all walk ahead of us as they leave the venue.

"I need to do a quick decompress and change before heading out."

"Is that all you have time for?" Jasper asks, wrapping his arms around my waist.

"Do you think we have time to fool around?" I fire back at him.

"Quinn, there is always time to fool around."

"That means you have to stay out later, otherwise the guys will never let you hear the end of it."

He smiles at me. One that settles everything inside of me because I get to love this man.

"You might have to prop my eyeballs open, but I think I can manage it."

I roll my eyes at him. "I don't know. I might have to take you home. I don't know if you can handle staying out that late, old man."

"Hey." He smacks my ass. "Is this you respecting your elders?"

I wink at him as I run to the dressing room.

"Damn straight. Let's go, Casper. Because I want to show you just how much I respect you."

"Hell, yeah."

Epilogue

"**A**re you going to sleep all day?" I press a kiss to Quinn's bare back.

"What time is it?" Her voice is scratchy with sleep.

"Nine."

"Nine?" Quinn groans. "You kept me up until two."

I smile against her warm skin, kissing each notch on her spine. "You didn't seem to mind last night."

Tugging the sheet down lower, I expose the swell of her ass. The bite marks I left there.

"A girl needs her beauty sleep."

She flips over, her naked body making my dick harden.

"I hear sex can also be good for you."

She waggles her fingers, beckoning me closer to her. "I have questions about the validity of that statement."

I shift her so she's under me, rocking into her.

"Sex burns calories, Quinn. It has to be good for you." She wraps her legs around me as I slide into her on a gasp. "I also hear orgasms are good for your skin."

"Must be why I'm always so radiant."

My moves are slow and tender as our mouths lock.

Before I know it, Quinn flips us and she's riding me. Watching the power she takes as she comes apart over me, taking me with her, is something I'll never take for granted.

With how chaotic our lives are going to be, I relish every quiet moment spent together.

Quinn starts to doze off after I clean her up. Tucking her back under the covers, I press a kiss to the crown of her head.

"I'll go make breakfast. Come out when you're ready."

She doesn't stir.

Grabbing my boxers and a sweatshirt, I pad out to the kitchen in our small cabin. With only a few weeks until Quinn's tour kicks off, we escaped to a small town in Montana—Pinecrest. I'd never heard of it, but Quinn found a place where we could hide away for a long weekend, just the two of us.

It's cold. After spending the night curled up in front of the fire, we moved into the bedroom.

The mountains spread out beyond the kitchen window as I start a pot of coffee and warm up a few cinnamon rolls from yesterday morning.

It's a weird feeling, being here right now. Having announced my retirement after finally—*finally*—winning the Stanley Cup, it's weird not to be playing with the season starting a few weeks ago.

My only job now is groupie to a pop star. It's going to take some getting used to, but thankfully I know what life on the road is like.

"Something smells good out here."

Quinn walks into the kitchen, robe tied around her waist and hair piled into a bun on top of her head.

"You could have slept in longer."

"Not when it smells so good out here."

I hand Quinn a cup of coffee and she take a long gulp.

"Morning." I hold my arm open for her to burrow into my side.

"Morning."

"So, what's on the docket for today?"

"Well, we could do horseback riding…" She trails off.

"Or?"

I try not to think about how much that would hurt. Me? On a horse? Something about that just doesn't feel natural.

"Or we could stay in."

"I like it."

"Order some room service. Curl up in front of the fire and play games."

"We are not playing Monopoly, Quinn."

"Oh, come on! I love it."

"And you should love me enough to know I do not want to play that game with you."

She hops up onto the counter, facing me, crossing one leg over the other. I do my best to ignore the way her robe parts, exposing her creamy thighs that I had wrapped around me last night.

"You're just mad that I'm a better player than you."

"There is no rhyme or reason to the game, other than it takes forever."

"We can play strip Monopoly," she says.

"That doesn't make it better." Although it does make it slightly more enticing. But I refuse to give in.

"You are such a poor sport."

I set down my coffee mug and step between her legs. "Quinn, I love you. I will eat Brussels sprouts for you and never make you eat cereal and always clean up after the cats. But Monopoly? We have to draw the line somewhere."

"Boo." Except she's smiling at me. "I think I saw

Connect Four in the living room. Would you want to play that?"

"I think I could muster up the energy to play that."

"We could also go for a hike too. The woman at the front desk said today would be a good day to go exploring before it gets too cold."

"I'm on to you, Quinn."

"What?" An innocent look is on her face.

"Throwing out Monopoly knowing I'll say no to playing, and then giving me things I can say yes to."

"I am doing no such thing."

I nip at her bottom lip. "Your face gives you away, baby."

"Nothing like working up a sweat before coming back and hitting the showers."

"Maybe we can grill out tonight, too, before watching some movies."

"I love it all, Jasper." She sighs, her warm breath ghosting over my lips. "Promise me we'll have nights like this on the tour."

"I don't know if we can do it here or in Switzerland, but I promise we'll curl up every night after your show and do whatever we want."

"We might have to catch a hockey game every now and then."

"What a hardship," I deadpan.

"You know, it won't be the same watching the Knights without you."

"Same. It's going to be weird for a while. But getting to watch you perform? It's the best trade-off."

"I mean, if you had to win the Stanley Cup as one last victory lap, you couldn't have asked for a better way to go out."

I smile down at her. "You know fans are going to lose

their minds when they see that we took the Cup into the studio with you."

"I hope they do."

It was the best way to spend my day with the Cup. We took it to the studio while Quinn recorded. After that? We put the cats in it, who did not like it. If we did something, the Cup came with us. Getting to celebrate with the person I love most was the dream ending to my career.

Quinn hops off the counter and takes my hand. "Why don't we go start this next chapter on a high note?"

"If you say Monopoly…"

"Jasper, if you think I'm going to take you into the bedroom to play Monopoly, I really have to teach you a few things, old man."

I slap her ass, running in after her.

"Then teach away."

But wait, Emily! They won the Cup!? Yes! Keep reading to get your bonus scene now…

Bode

"*Your Nashville Knights are Stanley Cup Champions!*"

"Fuck, yeah!" Marcus slams into me as the guys pile on around us.

"I can't believe it." Nothing but cheers ring out around the arena as our fans celebrate our win.

It's hard to believe we'll be hoisting the trophy over our heads in the next few minutes.

Something I've been dreaming about since I started playing hockey.

Winning the Stanley Cup.

The Nashville Knights are champions of the NHL.

I don't know if I'll ever get used to saying that.

"We did it!" Marcus skates over to pull Jasper into a hug as he comes onto the ice.

"I can't believe it." Jasper shakes his head. "Holy shit."

The crowd is raucous. Screaming, cheering, singing.

It's unbelievable.

"Champs, baby!" I say.

"I love you guys," Jasper says. "We did it. We finally did it."

"I wouldn't have wanted to play with anybody else," Marcus says. "I love you."

"Ditto." Dax laughs.

"You sure you want to retire?" Noah asks, ruffling Jasper's hair.

"Yeah, I'm sure. Can't beat going out on top."

"That's what he says." Graham snorts.

"Really?" Noah shakes his head.

"I blame you," I say. "You're a bad influence on him."

"He loves me." Graham kisses his cheek as the two of them share a moment together.

I gaze up into the stands. I know right where the family suite is. I can't wait to see everyone that's up there cheering us on.

I know Marcus's family is losing their minds. Graham and Noah's family got their own suite for tonight.

I can picture Stevie up there with our grandmas and Caleb. No doubt all of them are beside themselves with excitement.

I've never experienced a postseason run like this. I'm exhausted. I've pushed through aches and pains to keep going. To stay on the ice to get this moment right here.

I couldn't have done it without their support. Practice. Games. Travel. An insane schedule that meant I haven't spent enough time with them.

I can't wait to see them.

"Please stay in your seats for the presentation of the Stanley Cup." The announcer's voice echoes across the arena.

Excitement ripples through the team as the carpets are laid out and the Cup is brought onto the ice. I've never been this close to it. Sure, I've seen it in the Hall of Fame, but not for me.

Not for this group of guys that I consider family. We're

standing on the ice, championship hats now sitting on our heads as we wait for the ceremony to start.

The words all blur together as they congratulate Philly on a hard fought series. But before the Stanley Cup is presented, I'm presented with the Most Valuable Player trophy.

"Wait, they said my name?" I turn to look at Marcus.

"Hell, yeah!" He slaps me on the chest and pushes me over to where the trophy sits.

Holy shit. I never thought I would get this. Marcus? Yes. Me? I didn't think this night could get any better.

Then we're presented with the Cup. I can no longer hold back the tears. Being on top of the hockey world is a dream come true.

Coach Andrews passes Lord Stanley off to Marcus as captain for the first lap around the ice. I patiently wait my turn, watching as Marcus hands it off to Jasper.

Fuck. I can't believe he's retiring and this is how he's going out.

"Sorry, Mr. MVP," Marcus says as he skates to my side. "You're going to have to wait your turn."

I grin back at him. "Jasper deserves it."

I've never seen him look so happy.

"Have fun," Jasper says with tears rolling down his face.

"Yes!" I scream, kissing the metal as I hoist it over my head and skate around the ice. The Knights fans in attendance cheer as I do a lap.

You could see my smile from space. It's the shortest and best moment of my hockey career. Passing off the Cup to Graham, I skate back to the guys.

"Felt pretty good, didn't it?" Noah asks me. His eyes are wet as he watches Graham with the Cup.

"Fucking amazing."

And yet, it still won't compare to getting to *finally* hold Stevie and Caleb in my arms. As the last of the guys skate around the ice, families start to greet us. Marcus finds Harper who has tears streaming down her face. His entire family is clamoring for his attention.

Right behind them are the people I love most in the world. Stevie has Caleb in her arms. He's clinging to her as they step onto the ice.

She points her finger in my direction.

Caleb's eyes light up the minute he sees me. As he runs over on the carpets rolled out on the ice, I pick him up in my arms. "Hey, buddy."

I adjust the "Daddy" jersey he's wearing and check the headphones that cover his ears for the noise. "Daddy, you won!"

Who knew those words would bring me to tears? Watching the person Caleb is becoming might be one of the best things I never expected to experience.

My family—Stevie, Caleb, our grandmas, and the guys —means more to me than any trophy.

Stevie's beaming smile shines across the ice at me. Her feet are slow as she shuffles across the ice. Setting Caleb on his feet, I beckon her toward me.

"Hey, champ."

Grabbing her around the waist, I plant a kiss smack-dab on her mouth. I don't care that the cameras are flashing. I don't care who sees us. I want everyone to know what these people mean to me.

"I am so proud of you." Stevie cups my cheeks. Her hands are warm against the cold that blooms there. Her eyes are sparkling, even if I can tell she's looking a little pale. "I could have done with a little less stress though. I don't think it's good for me."

"I checked with the doctor. It's perfectly fine."

She throws her head back in laughter. A bright red Knights beanie hides her long unruly hair. She's repping her Adams jersey with pride. It's a bit big, but it hides the secret we're keeping from everyone. "Of course you did."

"Maybe next time this happens, it'll be less stressful."

Stevie shakes her head. "I don't think watching you play will ever get easier for me."

Caleb is now with Noah as he skates around the ice. Our grandmas are talking with Marcus's mom, giving us our space.

This is a night I will never forget. Being here, surrounded by everyone I love.

"I love you, Stevie. I'm so glad you're here."

"I don't care how miserable I feel; I would not miss this for the world."

We only found out a few weeks ago that we're pregnant. If we could have hidden the news from our grandmas, we would have. With their eagle eyes, they figured it out before we could even decide to tell them.

She's been miserable day and night. We couldn't get by without the two of them staying with us. At this point, I think they've claimed the pool house as their own and will never move out.

But I don't mind.

The two of them dote on Caleb, and I know they'll love our baby just as much.

"You look beautiful."

"You're lying."

I wrap my arms around her waist and pull her in close. The harsh lights of the arena glare down on us, but it doesn't matter. No one will ever hold a candle to this woman.

"You know I would never lie to you."

Her eyes sparkle. "Promise?"

I smile at her. "You have every one of my promises, Stevie. Making a promise to you is the easiest thing I'll ever do in my life."

"I love you, Bode." Tears wet her cheeks. "I don't think I'll ever forget this moment."

I thumb a tear away. "I won't either."

"At least until the next one."

"Knock on wood."

Stevie rolls her eyes at me. "You hockey players. So superstitious."

"Well, I'm hoping if that thing you just mentioned does come true, we might be doing it with a few more babies in tow."

"Let's get through baby number two before you put another one in me."

"As long as you know I want a houseful of kids."

Stevie snuggles into my arms as Noah and Graham bring Caleb back. He reaches out for me and I take him in my arms. "Yeah, yeah."

Noah and Graham go back to their families, leaving the three of us together.

As our grandmas come over to congratulate me, I soak up every bit of this moment. This is everything I never planned on having in life. I was fine on my own. Having people in my life meant they would leave me.

Turns out, I needed to find the right person.

Because life with Stevie and Caleb is something I could never have dreamed about. Each day with them is better than the last, and I can't wait to see what our future holds.

From playboy to family man…I have everything I need in life.

Right here in my arms.

Jasper

"I can't believe it's right there."

Marcus wraps his arm around my shoulders and pulls me in as Lord Stanley is brought in. Holy shit.

It's even prettier in person, seeing it gleam under the lights shining down on the ice.

Fuck. I still can't believe it. More tears come. Presentations and speeches are given before Coach Andrews passes the cup off to Marcus for his victory lap.

I thought it was loud before. It's nothing compared to when Marcus hoists that gleaming metal trophy over his head.

Fuck. I can't wait until that's me. There will be others in front of me, but I'm itching for that moment—knowing that the woman I love will be here to share in this moment with me.

Flashbulbs are firing off like crazy, the press snapping shot after shot of our captain going around the ice.

After his lap, he stops in front of me, passing the Cup off.

"Why me?" I'm shocked, staring at what's now half in my hands and half in Marcus's.

"You've earned it, Jasper."

"Thanks."

Taking a deep breath, I press my lips to the cool metal before lifting it over my head. It's hard to see through the tears still lingering in my eyes.

This is a moment I never thought would come. Something I've been dying to have, but now that it's here? I can't wait to share it with Quinn. It makes it all the sweeter.

As I turn toward our bench, the fans—the annoying, heckling fans who have sat behind me all season—are holding *Thank you, Hayes* signs.

I smile back at them as I finish my lap.

"YES!" I call out as all the fans snap pictures along the plexiglass.

The moment is gone in the blink of an eye as I pass it off to Bode, who was named MVP. He deserves it.

The wait is endless before families are allowed on the ice.

"You did it!" Quinn—sporting her usual Hayes jersey—slips and slides over the ice before leaping into my arms. Her baseball hat bumps into my forehead, falling off her head. "I am so proud of you."

Grasping my cheeks, she peppers my face with kisses. Our tears mix together.

"Quinn, I…"

It's hard to express what she means to me right now, at this moment. I know I would not be standing here if it weren't for her.

"I know, Casper." I smile at the nickname. "I know. I love you too."

"Can you believe we did it?"

The smile is going to be plastered on my face for weeks

to come. The Knights—the perennial losers in the league —are champions.

"There are going to be a lot of celebrations."

"Oh, I plan on it." If possible, my smile gets bigger. "It's because of you, my good luck charm."

"I don't know, you looked pretty good on your own."

I take the hat off my head and drop it onto hers. "Now you look even better."

"You sure this is what you want?" she asks. "You haven't announced you're retiring yet. You can still take it back."

"Positive." I nod my head. "I'm ready to be a groupie."

"You can be a groupie and play hockey at the same time."

"Nope. Full-time groupie status only. Besides, who's going to take care of the cats at the house?"

She shakes her head at me. "I still can't believe you bought me a red farmhouse."

I tuck a strand of blonde hair behind her ear. "We have to live somewhere."

"We are just fine in your condo."

"I'm ready to get out of the city. Maybe sing about fields being alive with the sound of music."

"I love you, Casper."

"I love you too, Bella." I kiss her, long and slow. The first and last time I'll ever get to do this after winning the Stanley Cup.

"Jasper. Genevieve. Can we get a picture of the two of you?"

I wrap Quinn in my arms as one of the photographers snaps a photo. It's hard to imagine I could ever be happier than I am right now, but I know each day with Quinn will get better and better.

I have everything I've ever wanted in life. No more

wondering about whether my life is complete. Hockey got me this far. Now, I'll get to be the person cheering Quinn on from the wings.

My life is damn good.

And I can't wait to see what it brings next.

Graham

"I can feel you vibrating," Noah says.

"Sue me. I'm antsy."

Standing with Noah's arm slung over my shoulder, I watch as Marcus passes the cup over to Jasper. The crowd goes wild. With it being his final season, it couldn't have ended better for him.

"It's even better than you think it is," he says.

"Hey. I want to decide for myself." I elbow him in the side. "Some of us don't know that yet."

He gives me a cocky grin. "I'll just tell you I'm right."

I shake my head at him, knowing he probably is. But I don't care.

Because my name is going to be etched on the Stanley Cup along with the rest of the Knights.

Damn. I didn't think seeing my name could get any cooler.

"I can't wait to celebrate tonight," Noah says.

I press a kiss to his cheek. "We're going to have a lot of fun."

That I can guarantee. Not only that, but the city is going to be insane tonight and I can't wait until we get to join in.

Jasper finishes his turn with the Cup and hands it off to Bode who was named the MVP of the finals. He deserves it. Without him, we wouldn't be standing here right now.

Bode skates up to me and passes over the Cup.

"Alright. Your turn."

Fuck. I've never felt anything so good in my hands. Fans are pounding their fists against the glass as I take a lap.

I press my lips to the cool metal before I skate over to Noah to hand it off to him. His eyes are wet with tears as I give it to him.

"You know," he says, "this might be the best win yet."

"Oh, yeah?" I grin back at him. I don't think anything could wipe the smile from my face tonight.

"Pretty damn special winning it with the person you love."

I can't help but kiss him. I don't care that the entire world is watching. This moment? It's just the two of us. I never thought this would be my life when Noah got traded to the Knights, but here we are. Finally doing what we said we always wanted to do.

Win the Stanley Cup together.

"Think someone got a picture of this?" He laughs.

Glancing around, I'm practically blinded by all the flashbulbs popping. "Oh, yeah."

"This is definitely going over the fireplace when we get a copy."

I shake my head at him as he skates off with the Cup, raising it high over his head. God, I love that man.

After everyone gets their chance with the Cup, families

are brought onto the ice. I skate over to mine, and my dad pulls me in for a tight hug.

"I am so proud of you, son," he says, voice clogged with emotion. "What a series you played."

I squeeze him back extra hard. "Thanks, Dad."

"How do you feel?" Mom asks, cheeks stained with tears.

Considering how many championships she's brought to the city of Denver, she knows this feeling.

"When I come back down to earth, I'll let you know."

"Sounds about right." She presses a kiss to my cheek. "We are so proud of you, Graham."

"He couldn't be the only one without a championship," Noah jokes, pulling me back into him.

"Noah!" his parents both yell at him at the same time.

"Just motivation for me to beat him," I say, hugging Noah to me.

"Does this mean you two are going to get married soon?" his sister, Piper, asks as she gives me a hug. "I want to make you my brother-in-law."

"One thing at a time, sis," Noah tells her. "We need to celebrate."

"Just don't go too hard," Tenley, Noah's mom, says. "I don't want you ending up on the cover of any tabloids."

"Mom," Noah groans. "I'm old enough to know better."

"Are you though?" I ask him. "Pretty sure I have to keep you in line."

"At least one of you does," his dad says.

"Oh, please. I'm the responsible one out of the two of us," Noah defends.

"Please. You know it's me," I say, knocking him in the side with my elbow.

"You just won the Stanley Cup and are arguing over who is more responsible." Dad shakes his head at us.

Noah looks at me. That look that tells me he loves me and we're going to be together for the rest of our lives.

I kiss him again. Because I can. "What can I say? I wouldn't have it any other way."

Marcus

Damn. Nothing feels better than this. Skating around the ice in our own arena lifting the Stanley Cup over my head?

It feels fucking amazing.

It'll be even better when our families get to come out onto the ice. Our fans are going wild in the stands. They've had our backs this entire season. Even through some dumb games and bad losses, they stuck by our side.

Not only do we get to bring this win home for us and our city, but for our fans.

Skating over to Jasper, I hand the Cup off to him. Winning it all in his final season after playing with the team his entire career?

What a better sendoff than that?

"Sorry, Mr. MVP," I tell Bode as I skate over to him. "You're going to have to wait your turn."

He grins back at me. "Jasper deserves it."

I don't know if it's possible, but the fans get even louder. Yeah, he really deserves this moment.

By the time he's skating back to hand the Cup off to

Bode, he's crying. Hell, I'm emotional because this will be the last time I ever get to play with him.

Before he can get far, I pull him in for a hug. "I'm going to miss you, man."

He claps me on the back. "You know I'm not going far, right?"

"Yeah, but when am I going to get to play with you again? I've never *not* had you on my team before."

"Just means you need to keep all these idiots in line."

"Oh, great." I roll my eyes at him. "I appreciate that. Really."

He pulls me in for another hug. "It's why you're the captain of the team."

"Yeah, yeah."

By the time everyone gets their turn on the ice, families are brought out.

Thank God. I don't think I could wait another minute to share this with Harper and the kids.

"You won! You won!"

Holding my arms open, three people come running at me. Hoisting Jamie into my arms, I wrap my arms around Sam and Sadie, as Harper looks on, tears running down her face.

"Can we get a puppy?" Jamie asks. An oversized championship hat sits on his head.

"Jamie! We said to wait," Sam hisses.

I bark out a laugh.

"Does that mean we're not getting one?" Sadie asks. "You said we could get one if you won."

"Girls, we'll visit that later," Harper says.

"Should we tell them?" I ask her, wagging my brows at her.

She looks at me, nothing but love and exasperation on her face. "You decide."

"Are we getting a dog?" Sam pulls on my jersey, looking way too excited.

"Please?" Jamie asks, turning his big blue eyes on me.

"We're getting a dog," I tell him.

"Yes!" both girls chant, before immediately discussing names.

Harper shakes her head, pulling me in for a kiss. "You are such a sucker."

I smile at her, stealing another peck. "What can I say? It's a good night for surprises."

"Oh, you want another surprise then?"

Now I'm confused. Another surprise?

It's been nonstop chatter about getting a dog for the last few months. Harper and I finally decided to get one once the playoffs were over. With school out and me being home, we'd have time to train him.

We have the perfect dog picked out that will be coming home this week. It was going to be the best surprise for the kids. Now I have no clue what she's talking about.

"What other surprise do you have?"

Grasping my neck, she pulls me close, lips against my ear. "We'll be adding to our family again in about, oh, seven and a half months or so."

"Wait…are you serious?"

Her eyes are glistening as her teeth dig into her bottom lip. "Yeah."

"Holy shit." I pull her in for a hug, burying my face in her neck.

"No cussing!" Sadie points out.

"I'll add a dollar to the jar," I say.

Because holy shit. We're having another baby?

It's something we talked about, but we were going to try after the playoffs. Get through getting a puppy.

Fuck. I don't think I could be any happier.

"Got room in there for your mother?" Mom pops up, and I have to wipe the tears from my face.

"Hey."

"I am so proud of you. I know Jamie and your father would be too."

My lip quivers. "I wish they could be here to see it."

"They're all watching." She pats my cheek. "What a game, Marcus. What a game."

"I can't believe we finally did it."

"Let me take Jamie. Hug your wife."

I pass him over and he struggles to get down to go play with Caleb. Having both arms free, I sweep Harper into my arms.

"You're really pregnant?" I whisper, not wanting anyone else to hear.

"Yes. Took the test last week and just got the results back from the doctor this morning. I didn't want to tell you until I knew for sure. You were a bit busy."

I smile at her. "I always have time for you. Fuck. I can't believe we're having another kid."

She drops her forehead to mine. "You think we can handle a dog and four kids?"

"As long as we have each other, we can do anything."

Dax

S tanley Cup Champions.

I can't believe it. As Noah brings the Cup to me, it's not sunk in yet. What a wild season it's been.

From getting suspended to being with Chloe, it's hard to believe I get to skate around the ice now. Not a single fan has left the arena yet. With each lap around the ice, it only gets louder.

As I take the Cup from Noah, the smile that stretches across my face is unmatched as I swing the silver trophy above my head.

"We Are the Champions" plays as I skate around the ice. Every single fan is singing along. This is a moment I won't soon forget.

I hand the Cup off and skate back over to the guys for another hug before our families are brought onto the ice.

"Feel good?" Graham asks.

"Amazing."

The smile on my face matches his.

"Glad we brought the win for the old man before he retires," Bode says.

"I can't keep up with you guys anymore," Jasper says, shaking his head.

"You're not going to go and start cheering for another team?" Noah asks, feigning shock.

"If I could flip you off, I would." Jasper gives him a shit-eating grin. "Knights for life."

I clap him on the shoulder. "We'll try and bring a few more home for you."

As the last of our teammates take their turn with the Cup, families are brought onto the ice.

"There's my champ!"

"Hey, Sunshine."

Sliding across the ice, Chloe leaps into my arms. "I am so proud of you!"

She peppers my face with kisses as I squeeze her to me.

"I couldn't have done it without you," I say, burying my face into her neck.

"You looked great out there. I mean, that goal in the second period to take the lead? Epic."

"Always my biggest fan."

"You got that right."

In my jersey, a jean jacket covered in Knights patches, a ball cap, and leggings, she has never looked more beautiful than she does right now.

And I can't believe that I get to share this moment with her.

"I still can't believe we did it," I say.

Chloe smiles at me, still in my arms. I'm not ready to let her go. She's the only thing grounding me in this moment.

"Now that it's happened, I feel like we need to start a list for you."

I throw my head back in laughter. "Oh, yeah? What kind of list?"

"I don't know. Things to accomplish now that I've won a Stanley Cup kind of list."

"What else is there to do?"

She shrugs a shoulder. "I don't know. Win a second one. Get MVP."

"Oh, easy," I say, nodding my head. "Piece of cake."

"Right? A snap of the fingers and it's done."

"You better make this happen, Sunshine."

"Nope. All you, Dax. This team is something special and I know you'll do it again."

"Hey, knock on wood," I say.

With Jasper retiring, it'll be anyone's guess as to how the team looks next year. Even though he's ready to hang up his skates, it's going to be a change for all of us.

Jasper's been on the team for nearly twenty years, and it'll be weird without him.

"I'm just lucky that I get to watch you play." Chloe's smile is warm and happy.

"Me too. Charms by Chloe is going to be the place to be in Nashville now after our win."

"Stop it." She swats at my chest, sliding down out of my arms.

"Hey, you know it will be. Everyone will be coming to get necklaces made to celebrate the Cup win."

She crosses her arms, pinning me with a look. "You're assuming I'm making something to celebrate the win?"

The corner of my mouth tips up in a smirk. "Like you don't already have something in mind."

She rolls her eyes. "Of course I do. I'll have to run it by the team first, but yeah, it'd be amazing if I can do something."

"I know you'll be able to."

After seeing how popular her hockey stick charms were after Genevieve bought one—Quinn, as we now know our friend's partner—the team reached out to partner with Chloe to make them exclusive to the team.

Business couldn't be going better for her, and I couldn't be prouder of her.

Sometimes I wish we still had our families by our side, but Chloe is everything to me. Her support has meant the world to me during this playoff run.

"Are you okay?" She cups my cheeks, eyes soft with emotion. It's like she knew exactly what I was thinking.

I thought it would be harder not to have my parents here by my side, but they've stuck by Duncan's version of events. Until I apologize to him, they won't talk to me.

I've made peace with it.

Because I have Chloe.

I nod. "I have you. That's all I need."

Have you read about the Black Diamonds? Check out my first hockey series now and pick up Best Kept Secret! And if you want what's next, you can preorder Fight For Us and add the series to your TBR today!

Acknowledgments

BOOK THIRTY IS OUT IN THE WORLD!

How in the world do I have THIRTY books out?! This was the first book of this type for me…an online romance, and I loved every minute of it. Jasper and Quinn's book flew out of me. I knew their story from the start of the series and loved getting to tease this throughout the rest of the guys' books. I hope you loved this book as much as I did, and I hope you enjoyed the little teaser of what is coming next…

Thank you to everyone in my bookish world, whom are too many to name! I love you all.

Thank you to all the readers who pick up my books and make this the best job in the world. You're the best!

Thank you for reading, and I hope to see you soon!
    <3 Emily

Also by Emily Silver

Nashville Knights

Game Misconduct

The Playmaker

Breakaway

Bar Down

Pinecrest, Montana

Fight For Us

Colorado Black Diamonds Hockey

Best Kept Secret

Best Laid Plans

Best of the Best

Best of Both Worlds

For a complete list of all my books, please visit my website.

Image by Tricia B @TheSmutFairy

After winning a Young Author's Award in second grade, Emily Silver was destined to be a writer. She loves writing inclusive stories, with strong heroines and the swoony men who fall for them.

A lover of all things romance, Emily started writing books set in her favorite places around the world. As an avid traveler, she's been to all seven continents and sailed around the globe.

When she's not writing, Emily can be found sipping cocktails on her porch, reading all the romance she can get her hands on and planning her next big adventure!

Find her on social media to stay up to date on all her adventures and upcoming releases!